SKY-PILOT
COWBOY

SKY-PILOT COWBOY

WALT COBURN

THORNDIKE
CHIVERS

This Large Print edition is published by Thorndike Press®, Waterville, Maine USA and by BBC Audiobooks, Ltd, Bath, England.

Published in 2004 in the U.S. by arrangement with Golden West Literary Agency.

Published in 2004 in the U.K. by arrangement with Golden West Literary Agency.

U.S. Hardcover 0-7862-6715-1 (Western)
U.K. Hardcover 1-4056-3038-8 (Chivers Large Print)
U.K. Softcover 1-4056-3039-6 (Camden Large Print)

The text of this Large Print edition is unabridged.
Other aspects of the book may vary from the original edition.

Set in 16 pt. Plantin by Liana M. Walker.

Printed in the United States on permanent paper.

British Library Cataloguing-in-Publication Data available

Library of Congress Cataloging-in-Publication Data

Coburn, Walt, 1889–1971.
  Sky-pilot cowboy / Walt Coburn.
    p. cm.
  ISBN 0-7862-6715-1 (lg. print : hc : alk. paper)
  1. Children of clergy — Fiction. 2. Fathers — Death —
Fiction. 3. Revenge — Fiction. 4. Large type books.
I. Title.
PS3505.O153S56 2004
  813′.52—dc22   2004049830

SKY-PILOT COWBOY

I

Galt Magrath was fifteen years old when cattle rustlers killed his father, Preacher Sam Magrath, the circuit rider. A grizzled old cowpuncher called "Hipshot" fetched the news to the round-up camp on the Pecos where Galt was hired out as horse wrangler.

For years afterward Galt could remember little, trivial details that went to make a picture of it all. The sort of peaceful setting that made the background for the news Hipshot fetched. Because it always seemed to Galt that from that evening on he quit being a boy and changed overnight into a man. So he always kept the picture of it in his mind.

It was near sundown when he drove the remuda into the rope corral. And the dust they kicked up made a haze in the air that reddened the sun as it dropped behind the skyline.

The cook, in his battered old hat, his run-over boots, his soiled floursack apron, limping around the open fire, lifting the Dutch-oven lids with a long-handled pothook. Cowpunchers lazing around. The wagon-boss figuring, or pretending to figure, with a stub of a pencil in a battered tally book he always carried in his vest pocket. The nighthawk rolling his bed. One of the cowpunchers tacking shoes on a horse. Old Hipshot walking over to the corral as Galt turned loose his sweaty horse. The jingle of the horse bells and how the sweat-streaked little roan rolled, turning plumb over on his round back twice. Which, as Galt remarked, made the roan pony worth twenty dollars more. Just a range expression used when a horse rolls over. And it was when old Hipshot didn't even grin that Galt first got the notion that something was the matter. Because old Hipshot grinned easy.

Hipshot was a range tramp who rode the grub lines from one camp or ranch to the next. And always paid for his grub with bits of range gossip. Hipshot was as welcome as the pony-express rider with the mail. He got his monicker not from any gun skill at shooting from his hip, but from his manner of standing; with his weight slouched on one long, bowed leg. When a horse stands with one hind leg resting like that, he stands "hipshot." And so whatever the old grubline rider's real name might have once been, it was lost long ago under the apt and descriptive Hipshot.

His long, leathery face looked solemn and there was none of the usual twinkle in his bright blue eyes. His drooping gray mustache gave him an almost sad look. And for the first time the old cowpuncher seemed at a loss for words of greeting. Just stood there, "hipshot."

Then Galt saw the book in Hipshot's gnarled hand. And though it had been many months since the boy had seen his father's service-worn Bible with its sewed-on buckskin jacket, he recognized it. And, staring at it, he saw that the pale yellow buckskin was stained with dried blood.

"Son, it's my job to tell yuh. I'm a hell of a pore, sorry hand at breakin' sad news. Preacher Sam's bin killed. The low-down, dirty skunks shot him fer no reason. Him as never packed a gun ner raised his hand ag'in' ary man. I come on his dead body and buried it as best I could, in the middle of the Staked Plains country. Nigh ten days ago, it was. The buzzards was commencin' to circle but hadn't lit yet. I had to ride a long ways before I found anything to mark his grave. . . . A wagon tire. His pockets had bin emptied clean. There was nothin' of his to fetch you exceptin' this." Hipshot held out the old Bible, with the bloodstains on its buckskin jacket.

Galt took the Bible and walked off down the river bank. Out of sight of camp he sat down on the ground and, with the old Bible in his hands, stared off into the afterglow, across the plains.

It was hard to name that heaviness that weighted his heart. Because it was not real grief. There had never been any sort of real love of father and son between the boy and the circuit rider who preached the laws of God far and wide across the cow country. For one thing, there was the big gap of years between their ages. And added to that was the bitterness left in Preacher Sam Magrath's heart when his wife had run off, taking Galt, then a boy of about eight or nine, with her. Galt had been too young to remember much about that flight north with his mother, who had bought passage with a wagon train. Sam Magrath had overtaken her at Dodge City. All the boy could remember was that his mother had wept a lot and he had cried with her and fought like a young cub panther when his father took him away from her. Back to Texas to farm him out with a family in San Antone. There he had gone to school until he was old enough to run away. He had started running away as soon as he could climb on the back of a horse. And they were always coming after him and fetching him back to town and school. And his father would read him long, dry, big-worded passages from the Book. None of which Galt had understood. Then, this last time he had run away, about a year ago, his father, instead of dragging him back to San Antone, had given him his school books and a long, fatherly sort of talk that had no Bible words in it, and had let him stay with the outfit. He had treated Galt like an equal and had even shaken hands with him when he left. And had left behind him a better understanding between them.

Galt remembered now how his father's stern, long-lipped face had softened as he talked. How, when he spoke of Galt's mother, he hadn't called her a bad woman, and his voice had a queer catch in it when he spoke her name. Mary, he had called her. And had likened her to a wild rose of County Kerry transplanted in a thorny wilderness. And that he had been punished by the Almighty because he had not practiced the words he preached of love and charity and forgiveness. And had blown his nose hard. And in the end he had taken Galt's hand in a strong grip and told him good-by and good luck. Then he had ridden away on his big brown mule with his Bible in his saddle pocket. To preach his words in a wilderness. A God-fearing man who rode unarmed across the Indian country and into frontier towns along the cattle trail to the north. Towns where badmen fought gun duels and filled unmarked graves in the boot-hill cemeteries. The warlike Comanches and Kiowas thought him crazy and so never harmed him. Cowboys, saloon men, gamblers, outlaws even let him alone. They called him by such names as Old Fire and Brimstone or Hell and Damnation or the Sin Buster, and tolerated him. And the grizzled, sinful, whiskey-drinking, gun-toting Hipshot had sometimes ridden with Sam Magrath across the plains and between them had been a strange sort of friendship.

The stars were beginning to come out when Galt walked back to camp. He found Hipshot and the grizzled range tramp gave him what few details there were to tell.

"From what the sign read, Galt, there was five-six, mebby, of 'em. The Lincoln County war in New Mexico has made outlaws of such tough cowboys as Billy the Kid and them as trails with him. They're dealin' plenty misery to the big outfits such as John Chisum's, the King of Seven Rivers. Might be it was Billy the Kid and his rustlers. Like as not they mistook Sam Magrath fer an enemy. They kill like a wolf pack. No man would set out to kill a harmless codger like Preacher Sam, who never packed a gun. They made a mistake."

"They robbed his pockets," said Galt quietly, his gray eyes hard as old steel under level black brows. "They left his body for the buzzards."

"That 'dobe ground makes hard diggin', son. And they was hazin' a bunch of stolen cattle. Rustlers don't pack shovels on their saddles."

"They killed my father. Murdered a man who never owned a gun of any kind in his life. They robbed his pockets and left his body for the coyotes and buzzards to fight over." Galt's soft drawl was still quiet. Too quiet to suit old Hipshot whose bright blue eyes covertly watched the boy's face in the reflection of the firelight. There was a long, awkward silence. Then Galt turned and walked back to the group around the campfire.

"I'd like to draw what money I got comin'," he told the wagon-boss. "I'll be saddlin' my private in the mornin'."

Then Galt Magrath walked off alone. When the fire had died down and the others had gone to bed, Galt crawled under his tarp and blankets. But he did not sleep. The bloodstained Bible made a lump under his head. And he tried to puzzle out in his mind why he felt so deeply about the loss of a father whom he had never loved. He could not understand his own feelings. Before dawn, when the nighthawk corralled the remuda, Galt was dressed and unbuckled his rope from his saddle. He caught his private horse, a line-backed dun he called Ranger, and a gotch-eared, flea-bitten pack horse named Button.

Hipshot took form in the gray dawn. "Figgered that mebby-so if you was travelin', I'd ride along. I could show yuh where Preacher Sam is planted, out acrost the Llano Estacada. That Staked Plains is hard country to find anything in."

Galt nodded. In that chilly gray dawn the old range tramp's awkward words put a queer lump in the boy's throat. You didn't expect any sort of sentiment in that hard-bitten old rascal and Galt knew that Hipshot was trying to cover a kind act with careless words. That old Hipshot knew Galt was starting out alone on a grim trail

14

across a strange land. And he was going along.

Nor did the old cowpuncher in any way belittle the boy's intentions; though Galt was only a gangling, loose-jointed youth of slender build and the six-shooter he packed looked as big as a cannon on his narrow flank. Though in many ways he thought and acted like a grown man. Like now, setting out to trail down the men who had murdered his father. He went about the grim business quietly, without words. That was Galt Magrath's way. And it pleased old Hipshot and the other cowhands.

There was no handshaking, no farewells. Galt and Hipshot simply rode off into the sunrise, leading their bed-laden pack horses. . . .

A norther was sweeping the bleak, dismal, waterless stretch of desolation known as the Llano Estacada, or Staked Plains. It was early spring and the raw wind bit into the marrow of a man's bones. Galt's face was bluish with cold and his legs felt numb. Old Hipshot must have suffered more than did the boy, for his blood was thin and his bones were brittle. But neither of them complained.

Not that Galt had any special hankering to see the lonely grave of Preacher Sam. When a

15

man died, he was buried, and that was an end to it. And a grave was something you marked with a rock or a wooden cross, like the Mexicans did, or located it by a tree or some similar landmark. Then you rode away from it. Cowpunchers aren't long on sentiment. At least they let on thataway. And Galt's ways were the ways of a Texas cowhand. And you didn't expect to find any sentiment in the tough make-up of old Hipshot.

Nevertheless, Hipshot, acting as guide across that hundred-mile strip of wilderness, bent their trail to the north a little, instead of due west, where they would strike their first water at the Horsehead Crossing on the Pecos. Galt reckoned that it was something besides sentiment that was turning Hipshot into the teeth of a snow-spitting norther to look at a grave. And he was right.

Towards night, the dry snow stinging their slitted eyes and making their cheek muscles stiff, Hipshot halted beside a place marked by twisted pieces of iron and steel that had been parts of two wagons. Charred bits of wood showed in the thin skift of snow that covered the bare ground that was too arid to grow even greasewood or other brush.

"What do you make of it?" asked Hipshot,

16

as their horses turned rumps to the wind.

"Two wagons burned," said Galt. "Fairly recent." He looked around for graves but saw none. "Injuns, Hipshot?"

"No. And it wasn't ary wagon train because there was only the two wagons burned. It was here I got the wagon tire I taken to mark Preacher Sam's grave. And the sign was fresh around here then. I burried the scattered bones of half a dozen men. There was six skulls, to tally by. No Injuns killed 'em, because they hadn't bin scalped. I made a hole and buried all the bones in the one grave. Then I taken the shovel I'd found here and tied onto the wagon tire and drug it back to where I'd left Preacher Sam covered sorta makeshift, not ten miles from here. And the tracks of his mule led almost direct from here. Other sign told me that he'd bin here with this outfit. Probably camped with 'em when they was wiped out. He got away and they trailed him. The renegades that killed Preacher Sam had an almighty good reason fer doin' so. Preacher Sam Magrath knowed too much. He had to be killed to stop his tongue."

"Driftin' across the country," guessed Galt, "he stopped overnight with this outfit."

"That's it, son. And bad luck overtook him. Nobody had reason to kill Preacher

17

Sam. That's what puzzled me when I come on his dead body. This explains it."

"I wonder what outfit it was, Hipshot, that was wiped out."

"It was a pool herd from over on the San Saba, east of San Angelo. Headed up the trail for Montana. I don't reckon you knowed the outfit. It was a mixed herd and a queer 'un, and some of the men was little better than the rustlers who wiped 'em out. I camped with 'em on the North Concho about three weeks ago. There was ten men in the outfit. They didn't act none too hospitable and I only stayed one night with 'em. Mind the tally I taken of 'em then. Ten men, includin' the cook and hoss wrangler. And I planted six skulls. That leaves four."

"Four that got away," nodded Galt.

"Four out of ten didn't git killed here. But they might have bin trailed and shot in the back like Preacher Sam was. Or they throwed in with the rustlers that raided the trail herd. It's my guess that more than one tough gent in the pool outfit was in cahoots with the rustlers that come down outa New Mexico and waylaid the outfit. That's my guess. And I reckon it's as good as any."

"You'd know the ones that didn't git killed here?"

18

"I'd know 'em by sight. One or two, mebbyso, by name," replied Hipshot cautiously. "I'll know 'em when we cut their sign."

They made a dry camp that night at the grave of Galt's father. The grave marked by a fire-blackened wagon tire. There was no water except a little they carried in their canteens. No wood for a fire. Bull chips and buffalo chips made a hotter fire, however, than wood, for cooking the strong, black coffee and meat. But there was no cheering blaze to sit by. The bitter wind seemed all the colder for the darkness and the fine, hard snow stung like frozen sand. They crawled under their blankets.

Hipshot talked through the darkness and Galt listened and learned from the old range tramp's store of wisdom.

"Three-four men, mebbyso, trailed Preacher Sam because he knowed too much. And they killed him where they ketched up with him. Them three-four was only part of the rustler outfit, and the one that fired the only bullet needed to kill your daddy, wasn't no more guilty than the rest of the gang. Like as not they somehow drawed lots to see who'd do the actual killin'. It wasn't a pleasant job to kill an unarmed circuit rider, who, a few hours ago, had read to 'em out of his Bible. The man that shot Preacher Sam ain't noways proud of hisself. But he's no more guilty than the others. On the trail, every bullet counts and they saved ca'tridges by usin' only one bullet to stop Preacher Sam from spreadin' the news.

"So you see, son, yuh can't go trackin' down mebbyso twenty men and killin' 'em. Anyhow Sam Magrath wouldn't want it thataway. He didn't believe in gun fightin'. He wouldn't want his own son, his only son, turnin' killer."

Hipshot's words died away in the whine of the norther and Galt did not break the silence between them. Galt understood now why the old cowhand had bucked the bitter cold wind and had taken them miles out of their way to camp by the grave of Preacher Sam Magrath.

After a time Galt could hear old Hipshot muttering and moaning a little in his sleep. Again the buckskin-covered Bible with Sam Magrath's blood staining it, was under Gait's head. And sleep came only after a long time to the boy who had spread his blankets and tarp near the grave of his father. But with that reluctant sleep came a certain sort of peace of mind. A peace that had to do with the wise range philosophy of old Hipshot.

II

Hipshot grinned and dug his thumb roughly into Galt's ribs as they stood reading the dodger tacked to the outside front wall of the Post-office. It had been three years since the night they had camped beside the grave of Sam Magrath. And those three years had cemented a strong friendship between the boy and the old range tramp. Though time seemed to have made no change in Hipshot, it had changed Galt into a well-made youth who looked older and acted older than his eighteen years.

Hipshot, a little drunk, tapped the name of Billy the Kid with a forefinger as he stood, weight slouched hipshot on one long leg.

"A year gone by since Sheriff Pat Garret of Lincoln County killed that little buck-toothed bushwhacker *buscadero* you and me knowed as Billy the Kid. Eh, Galt? This 'un

21

NOTICE!

TO
THIEVES, THUGS, FAKIRS AND BUNKO-STEERERS

Among Whom Are

J. J. HARLIN, alias "OFF WHEELER;" SAW DUST CHARLIE, WM. HEDGES, BILLY THE Kid, Billy Mullin, Little Jack, The Cuter, Pock-Marked Kid, and about Twenty Others:

If Found within the Limits of this City after TEN O'CLOCK P.M., this Night, you will be Invited to attend a GRAND NECKTIE PARTY.

The Expense of which will be borne by

100 Substantial Citizens.

Las Vegas, New Mexico.   March 24th, 1882.

The dodger tacked outside the Post Office.

listed here is a cheap imitation of the killer we knowed; when we follered the stolen San Saba trail herd into New Mexico and found the cattle sold and the rustlers scattered; and learned at Fort Sumner that Billy the Kid couldn't have bin mixed up in the killin' of Preacher Sam because he was in jail at the time." He tapped the brand new dodger with his bony forefinger.

"What day of the month do you reckon this is, Galt?"

"March the twenty-fourth."

"And what time might it be by the hour and minute hands of that silver stem-winder I won off that tin-horn at Santa Fe?"

Galt looked at the heavy silver watch. "Half an hour past seven and time we had supper."

"Supposin' you mosey along to the eatin' place while I hi'st just a light 'un er two to whet my appetite?" Hipshot's bright blue eyes were as pleading as his drawling voice.

"We had our last square meal sometime yesterday, Hipshot. You've already poured a quart of redeye into an empty belly. I like to never got the jail bars filed the last time you painted a town red after the likker splashed around in your empty belly. If you git jailed we'll both likely miss the necktie party the Vigilantes are plannin'. Let's eat. Grub

23

makes a foundation for this Las Vegas forty-rod whiskey."

"You preach like your daddy usta. But right you are, son. We'll have the waiter fetch a pint to tone up the coffee and flavor the soup with. And join up with the one hundred Substantial Citizens."

Standing in his habitual peculiar fashion, Hipshot closed an eye and again studied the names on the dodger. Then he and Galt pushed through the gathering crowd and on down the street.

Las Vegas was teeming with life. Spur-dragging cowboys swaggered and lurched along the street. Others rode up and down, mostly in groups of two or more. Many of them were partly drunk. Now and then a cowboy let out a wild whoop as he bucked his horse down through the crowd. Or some rider would empty his gun at the stars that were beginning to show in the sky. Saloons were crowded. Now and then some cow-hand would call Hipshot by name and try to drag him into a saloon for a drink. But the grizzled range tramp shook them off.

"Got to git grub. Us Substantial Citizens can't work on an empty belly. Come on, Galt."

A tall, wide-shouldered man with graying straw-colored hair and bleak eyes and a hawk nose almost collided with them as he lurched out of the swinging half-doors of a saloon.

Galt felt Hipshot's left hand grip his arm, pulling him back. Saw the old range tramp's right hand drop to the cedar butt of his long-barreled six-shooter.

The man with the pale eyes stiffened, and his hand dropped to his gun. Galt's gun hand closed over his own weapon. For a long, tense moment Hipshot and the big man eyed one another with deadly appraisal.

Then a crowd spewed out of the saloon, unaware of Hipshot or the other man. They jostled and pushed and the big man was carried along with them as they headed across the street.

When the man with the bleak blue-gray eyes, eyes that were a milky color, blood-shot, dangerous, had been lost in the crowd, Hipshot's hand slid his half-drawn gun back in its holster.

"Who was he?" asked Galt.

"Him?" Hipshot, who had gone cold sober in that tense moment, relaxed limply and the color came back into his lean, leathery face.

"Him? I thought fer a minute I knowed him. Can't recollect his name." He took

Galt's arm in a bony grip and moved on.

Galt asked no more questions. But he knew that Hipshot lied and he felt hurt because of it.

At the restaurant, Hipshot shook hands heartily with a short, thick-set man with a wide grin and wintry gray eyes. He had iron-gray hair and a ragged mustache stained at the corners from tobacco smoke.

"Galt," said Hipshot, "shake hands with the best damned cowman that ever piloted a trail herd outa Texas. Jeff Curtis of the Mill Iron, unless some other outfit has hired him away from 'em. Jeff, this is Galt Magrath. His daddy was Preacher Sam, the circuit rider."

"The hell," said Jeff Curtis, as he shook hands. "I knowed your father. A good man, even if he couldn't make a believer outa me. Didn't he die off?"

"Got killed," volunteered Hipshot, "about the time the San Saba Pool herd got lost crossin' the Staked Plains. You recollect?"

Jeff Curtis's grin faded and his eyes looked colder than before. "I got reason to recollect."

"Didn't know there was ary Mill Iron cattle in the pool herd," said Hipshot carelessly, his eyes bright.

26

"There wasn't." And the look in his eyes forbade questioning. Galt saw Hipshot's head nod almost imperceptibly as the two men eyed one another.

"I'm goin' up the trail with a big herd," said Jeff Curtis. "I could use you at top wages, Hipshot."

"You'd have to hire Galt to ride herd on me. He's kinda taken up Preacher Sam's job of reformin' me, where Sam left off. Last outfit we worked for, I stuck 'er out damn near six months. I was gatherin' moss to beat hell. And I ain't bin on a good drunk in . . . how long has it bin, son?"

"It's five weeks this comin' Sunday since I sawed you out of the Socorro jail," grinned Galt, and Jeff Curtis chuckled.

"Galt packs along a file like some fellers pack a Bowie knife," explained Hipshot. "Now I'd swore it was three months since I got chawed up by them Socorro jail bedbugs. Time shore flies. Not much of a recommend this young button gives a man, eh, Jeff?"

"I kin use you both," said Jeff Curtis.

"I'll talk 'er over with Galt. We just got to town and I got a leetle pokerin' to do. Feel lucky. We'll ketch your outfit in a few days. Where'll you be by then?"

"We're camped on the Canadian River.

27

Expect to be there a week. We're goin' all the way to Montana. I rode over here on a little business."

"Connected with that dodger tacked up at the Post-office?" questioned Hipshot.

Jeff Curtis grinned faintly and shook his head. "They forgot to put your name on their list, Hipshot."

"Hell, Jeff, I'm one of them Substantial Citizens," grinned Hipshot as the trail boss moved off.

But as they sat down at a table, Galt noticed that the old range tramp so placed his chair that his back was to the wall and he commanded a view of both front and rear doors.

"Don't pay no attention to Jeff's hoorawin', son," he said.

Galt shook his head, and made some joshing remark that put Hipshot at his ease. Just the same, Galt knew that the grizzled cowhand was a little uneasy, and his keen blue eyes were restless.

Hipshot was no saint. He had, in his years of wandering, unrolled his bed at many strange camps and had ridden with all manner of men. And though Galt was aware that Hipshot, since the two had become partners, had always made a point of avoiding evil company, there had been a few

28

times when they had camped with men who were obviously outlaws. And they had always treated Hipshot as one of them. And accepted Galt as being vouched for because he rode with Hipshot. It was not Galt's way to ask questions. He was no judge of Hipshot or any other man. It paid to mind your own affairs if you wanted to steer clear of trouble. It was none of Galt's affair if Hipshot had ridden with outlaws and rustlers. After all, the line separating the rustler from other cowhands was at times almost invisible. Some of the biggest outfits in the West were called hard names.

They were eating when a group of perhaps half a dozen men came into the restaurant. They were sober. Two of them carried sawed-off shotguns. Their eyes studied every man in the room. Galt saw Hipshot go tense as one of them said something to the others in a low tone, then walked over to the table where Hipshot and Galt sat at supper.

Hipshot seemed to make a point of keeping both hands in plain sight, fork in one hand, table knife in the other, upright in his fists that rested on the table edge. He looked up at the tall, handsome man who might have been part Mexican. A majority of the citizens of Las Vegas were New Mexi-

cans, descended from the first Spanish set-
tlers.

"Que horas son, señor?" asked the man,
smiling faintly, his dark eyes looking from
Hipshot to Galt, then back to the older man.

"Tell Judge Ortega what time it is by the
stem-winder, Galt," said Hipshot.

Galt consulted the big, silver watch. He
looked up at the tall New Mexican.

"Ten minutes till nine, señor," he said.

The man took his own watch from a vest
pocket, looked at it, nodded, then turned
and walked away. He joined the group near
the door and they left the place as quietly as
they had entered.

Hipshot poured some whiskey into his
empty coffee-cup and drank. He wiped his
drooping gray mustache with the back of his
hand and grinned wickedly at Galt.

"Judge Ortega give me my choice of
huntin' a new climate or gittin' free board
and room at his 'dobe jail once, a few years
back. He's the law around Vegas. Nice feller,
from what I hear tell of him. Finish your
puddin', son. I'll settle my grub with what's
left in the bottle."

But Galt had no appetite for the dish of
bread pudding and its pink sauce. The Vigilantes had given them a grim warning. Galt
paid the bill and they went outside. . . .

Wary and on guard as Hipshot was, it was Galt who first caught sight of the big man with the hawk nose and bleak, pale eyes. And there was no time to waste giving his companion warning. The big man was going for his gun, there in the street at the hitchrack.

Galt's gun roared. He shot from the hip. A snapshot. The heavy lead slug made a freak hit, striking the big six-shooter in the man's hand. The gun exploded with a roar as it was torn from the man's hand.

Hipshot, bent forward at the waist, was shooting. Not at the big man with the pale, bleak eyes, whose face had a twisted, startled expression. But at two other men at the hitchrack. One of them slumped to the dirt in a limp heap, the horses at the hitchrack kicking dust around him as they reared and lunged at their tie ropes. The other man tried to crawl into his saddle but the horse jerked away. The man was wounded and in the light that came from the restaurant Galt caught a glimpse of a blood-smeared face. The man's foot hung in the stirrup and the bolting horse dragged him a ways, kicking at the struggling form hung to the stirrup. Then the man's boot came loose from the stirrup and the horse bucked down the street. While the big man with the pale eyes

31

swung into the saddle and was gone in a moment.

The two men Hipshot had hit lay motionless in the street. Hipshot grabbed Galt's arm and shoved him through the gathering crowd. It had happened so suddenly that nobody had quite gotten the details of it all. Save for the yellow blots of light that came from the restaurant and saloons, the street was in the shadow of night.

So quickly did Hipshot move with Galt that the identity of the participants in the brief gun fight was lost in the confusion. They worked their way through the crowd unobtrusively and went on down the street. Once away from the scene of the fight, they slipped fresh cartridges in their guns, ejecting the empty shells that were still warm. And in a few minutes they were in front of the Post-office. Here Hipshot paused in front of the Vigilante dodger. With the lead of a .45 cartridge he ran a heavy line through two names on the list. Marking off Little Jack and The Cuter.

"I'll git a bottle and meet you at the shed where we left our horses, son. If I don't show up in half an hour, you pull out without me and keep a-ridin'."

"Nothin, doin', Hipshot. We're pardners and . . ."

"We got a long ride ahead of us to the Mill Iron camp on the Canadian. I need oil fer my j'ints. Have the horses ready." And he was gone in the crowd before Galt could stop him.

Galt made his way to the shed at the edge of town where they had left their horses at a Mexican's place. The Mexican was a friend of Hipshot's and had cared well for their horses. As was their custom when visiting a town they always put up at some friend's place. Hipshot seemed to have such friends all over the country.

The Mexican helped Galt load the two beds on the pack horses. He asked no questions and Galt volunteered no information. It was almost ten o'clock when they finished and Hipshot had not shown up. Galt became uneasy as more minutes went by and there was no sign of the range tramp.

Whiskey was Hipshot's one weakness. Give him one drink and he would not stop until he had finished his drunk. In spite of all obstacles. And the stuff made him too bold, too reckless, too careless.

Ten o'clock. Galt told the Mexican to wait here with Hipshot's saddled horse and the two pack horses. Then he mounted and rode up the crowded street. There was more of a crowd than ever. Especially in front of the Post-office. Galt reined up and scanned the crowd for a glimpse of Hipshot. But the long-legged range tramp was nowhere in the crowd. But luck favored Galt. He spotted Jeff Curtis with some cowboys at the edge of the crowd. And dismounting, he led his horse to where the trail boss was standing.

"I've lost track of Hipshot," he said.

"The Vigilantes haven't. We was lookin' for you, button. Thought they'd grabbed you, too. Come along."

Jeff Curtis and his men mounted their horses. At the trail boss's orders, Galt got Hipshot's horse and met them at the end of the street.

"Wait here for us. Keep out of sight. We'll be back directly with that ol' rannyhan. . . ."

Galt waited as Jeff Curtis and his cowboys rode back up the street. It seemed like hours before he saw them coming back, their horses on a run. Hipshot was riding behind Jeff Curtis. As they slid to a halt, old Hipshot was on the ground. A long-legged leap and he was on his waiting horse.

"Meet you on the Canadian, Jeff," he said, as he and Galt spurred away, the Mill Iron men guarding their escape. They picked up the waiting pack horses and left town on a high lope.

They had covered several miles before

they slacked to a road trot. Hipshot chuckled softly as he pulled a bottle from inside his flannel shirt. He took a long drink, then corked the bottle.

"Never did like that two-bit town of Las Vegas," he complained. "From now on, I take my trade elsewheres. I was buyin' a bottle, peaceful as sin, when them Substantial Citizens collared me. Not Judge Ortega, because he's level headed. And his watch kep' the correct time accordin' to our stem-winder I won off that tin-horn at Santa Fe.

"They bundled me off and put me in a house under guard. But as they herded me outa the saloon I ketched sight of Jeff astandin' near the door. Jeff Curtis is a friend that don't quit in a tight.

"So I ain't su'prised when him and his boys take me away from the three guards. I got my gun back. And what's more, never spilled a drop er busted a bottle." Hipshot chuckled and took another drink. Then he looked at Galt from under the slanted brim of his hat.

"Thought I told you to hightail it if I didn't show up by nine-thirty or thereabouts?" he growled.

"Mebbyso the stem-winder is losin' time or stopped on me," replied Galt.

"Button," said Hipshot, "I've said it before and I told it to Jeff Curtis when we rode double down the street. You'll do to take along."

At a safe distance from Las Vegas and her Substantial Citizens, as Hipshot referred to now and then in no uncertain terms, they made camp. And the old range tramp proceeded to finish his drunk alone.

It was no new experience for Galt to nurse the old rascal through one of these drinking bouts, sober him up on strong black coffee spiked with fiery red chili peppers the size of a pea, and listen to his moaning.

It took about twenty-four hours. Sober, a little shaky, Hipshot led the way once more, heading eastward, towards the Canadian River. Old Hipshot reckoned it would be about two hundred miles to where the Mill Iron herd was camped.

Galt reckoned they had covered about half that distance across a country that was none too safe on account of roving war parties of Indians that were out after wagon trains or small parties of travelers. They rode at night and hid out during the day. It was toward dusk when they sighted three men driving a bunch of horses. They came from the direction of the Canadian.

"How many horses they drivin', Galt?"

"Close to seventy-five head, I'd reckon."

"And you won't miss the tally by three head, son. They're hazin' 'em along almighty fast, fer honest travelin'. It's my guess that them three gents has stole that bunch of horses. And they ain't Injuns. Ain't enough of 'em to be Injuns. Them's white men. And they'll be comin' our way. Cache the pack horses and we'll look them jaspers over."

The country was broken, spotted with brush. Galt hid the two pack horses as best he could, then rode back to join Hipshot who had been watching through a pair of army field glasses.

"Never steal an off-colored horse," grunted Hipshot, as if musing aloud. "I'd know that piebald spotted sorrel anywheres. I've watched Jeff Curtis cut cattle on that geldin' without touchin' a bridle rein. Son, we've horned into somethin'. I know that hoss. And bad as the light is, I spotted three-four more Mill Iron hosses in that bunch, that was in my string when I worked fer Jeff a few years ago. Take the other side of this brushy draw. Git in behind that biggest brush patch on the far side. Git your horse outa sight so's he won't git hit by stray bullets. Lay flat on your belly and when I open the jackpot from this side, you let 'em have it from where you are. We're takin' them horses away from them three low-down hoss thieves. You foller my lead in whatever I do. I'm givin' 'em a chance to surrender peaceful."

Galt nodded without asking foolish questions. He had seen Hipshot kill two men back at Las Vegas, and he knew that the grizzled range tramp was ready to do more killing if he had to. It was not for a young hand like Galt to question the methods of an old-timer.

Galt hid his horse and took his stand behind a patch of brush on the side of the long draw. It was getting dusk as the three men came into the draw with the horses. One man riding in the lead. The other two driving the horses behind him.

In the dim light Galt thought he recognized the man riding in the lead, though the distance was over a hundred yards and the light was bad. But the man with the bleak eyes and hooked nose, back at Las Vegas, was a big man and he'd worn a high-crowned black hat and a light-colored shirt. The big man riding up in the lead answered that description. Galt had not asked Hipshot questions regarding the name or reputation of the man. And Hipshot had seemed to avoid mentioning him.

Now, from the brush across the draw

where Hipshot was hiding in ambush, there came a puff of gun smoke and the loud crack of the old range tramp's saddle gun. The bullet kicked up dust a few feet in front of the man riding ahead of the horses. And as the man jerked his gun, Hipshot's voice cut through the echoes of his warning shot.

"Stand your hand, Pecos! Claw for your gun and I'll shoot you outa the saddle. We got you three hoss thieves acrost a barrel. Take our orders or we'll kill the three of yuh. We mean business. We want them horses and we're takin' 'em, regardless. You're listenin' to Hipshot."

The man Hipshot had called Pecos had his six-shooter in his hand. He sat his horse with his weight in one stirrup, tense, undecided. Then Hipshot called out again.

"One of you boys acrost the draw drop a shot over that big son's head, just to let him know I ain't alone and this ain't a bluff. Put a hole in that black hat."

Galt's saddle gun rested on a rock. It was still light enough to see the sights. Though the black hat was a small target, it showed plain. And Galt was a good shot, steady of nerve, confident. His finger pressed the trigger. As the lead slug tore through the top of the high-crowned black hat, the big man ducked. Hipshot's mocking laugh came

39

from the far side of the draw.

"What'll it be, Pecos? Do we leave you three snakes for the buzzards or will you give us these Mill Iron hosses peaceful?"

"You win, you damned, double-crossin' son of a snake. Turn the ponies loose, boys. He's got us foul. He wins this jackpot but the game ain't ended. Come on, men!"

"Not so damned fast, Pecos. I ain't fool enough to give you ary chance to trail us and turn the trick on us. Throw away your saddle guns, all three of yuh. You two other gents will kindly ride around to near where Pecos is. Move fast. . . . That's the idee. Now, Pecos, you and the gent on the blue roan will dismount and unsaddle. Turn your horses loose. Give your saddle guns to the gent on the bay hoss. He'll fetch them guns to me and drop 'em on the ground. Pecos, you and the gent on the blue roan unsaddle and turn your ponies loose. If you don't, we'll kill the three of yuh."

"You can't set us afoot out here a hundred miles from nowhere! This is Injun country!"

"Is it? Ain't that hell, again? I ain't settin' you plumb afoot. I'm leavin' you one stout horse between yuh. From here on to Las Vegas, you kin take turns ridin' and walkin'. If the Injuns git yuh, then they're savin' them Substantial Citizens of Las Vegas the

40

trouble of hangin' yuh. All right, unsaddle. Time's goin' to waste. You on the bay hoss. While Pecos and the other skunk is settin' theirselves afoot, you drift that bunch of hosses back the way you come. Galt, when the hosses go through the gap, you take charge of 'em. Git your pony and throw the pack hosses in with this bunch. If Pecos or either of his two amigos make a move to take a shot at yuh, I'll kill the three of 'em. But I reckon you kin make it without them even seein' you. Reckon?"

"You bet!" called Galt. He wormed his way to where he had left his horse, got the two laden pack horses, and gathered the loose horses as they drifted through the gap between two hills at the head of the long draw. When he bunched them, he rode back. In time to see Pecos and one of the men, striking out on foot, a hundred yards or so behind the man on the bay horse who was headed towards Las Vegas. Hipshot joined Galt.

"Like as not we should have killed Pecos Moss and them other two renegades," Hipshot said, scowling through a leathery grin. "Because as long as Pecos is alive and kin handle a gun, he's dangerous. But we just can't go killin' folks from the bush. Ever hear of Pecos Moss, son?"

41

"Since I kin remember. He's plenty bad. It was him that —"

"That we met in Las Vegas, yep. And his gun hand is wropped in a rag. He's bad medicine. It was Pecos Moss that was ramrod of the San Saba Pool trail herd. You might as well know now as later, when it might be too late. He knows by now, I reckon, that you're Preacher Sam's son. And like as not he might be able to tell how Preacher Sam got killed. But you ain't goin' back after Pecos Moss now. We're takin' these Mill Iron hosses to the camp on the Canadian."

III

The next day they were camped on water with the horses. They had kept them moving all night and now as the horses watered and grazed, Galt watched them while Hipshot got some sleep. At noon Hipshot would go on guard while Galt slept a few hours. At dusk they would again be moving.

Galt was dozing in the saddle when half a dozen armed men on leg-weary, sweat-marked horses rode up. Their guns covered Galt. A tall, well-made young cowhand, not many years older than Galt, seemed to be the leader. They all rode Mill Iron horses and Hipshot had told Galt like as not some of the Mill Iron men would be showing up.

"If there was a tree handy," said the young cowboy, whose bloodshot, black-colored, slitted eyes stared at Galt, "we'd string you up here. Make a gun play and I'll be glad to gut-shoot you. Scatter out along the crick, men, and gather in the others. Take no chances. Kill 'em where you find 'em. We'll learn 'em to run off our remuda."

Then Hipshot rode into view, waving his hat as a sign of peace. He rode up under the guns of the Mill Iron cowhands. They eyed him with cold suspicion as they recognized him. The young cowboy with the black eyes scowled.

"At your old game, eh, Hipshot? You'll hang this time."

"There ain't a tree in fifty miles of here, young feller. And you better put off the necktie party till Jeff Curtis gits here. And put up your guns. Me and my pardner Galt Magrath never stole these horses."

"Take their guns," snapped the young cowpuncher. "Don't let that horse-thievin' old Hipshot talk you out of it. I'll ride herd on the young 'un. We're hangin' 'em to the first tree we come to. We all know that Hipshot's as crooked as a snake's tracks. And the button looks like a sheep-killin' dog to me. Take their guns and tie 'em to their saddle horns. Uncle Jeff will find their carcasses a-hangin' to a tree limb when he comes along."

"The young rooster that's doin' all the

loud crowin'," said Hipshot as he and Galt were being tied to their saddles, "is kind of a shirt-tail cousin of Jeff's. His name is Lon Coulter and he ain't lyin' when he says he'll kill a man. I knowed his daddy Joe Coulter before he died of lead poisonin'. Lon comes by his onery ways plumb natural. Likewise his nasty tongue fightin'. So do what he says, Galt, and say nothin'. Jeff will set him back where he belongs when he gits to camp. Unless you want the hide skinned off your back, young Lon, you better treat me and Galt like we was white folks."

"I'm ramroddin' this spread," sneered Lon, his dark face flushing hotly.

"So it seems," said Hipshot. "It was Joe Coulter's tongue that got him killed in San Antone. That and his awkwardness with a gun. Be careful you don't die of the same symptoms. Jeff's goin' to turn me and Galt loose when he gits here. And I don't like to be called dirty names. Neither does my pardner. As the law says, when they ketch yuh, anything you say will be remembered ag'in' yuh."

"You oughta know, mister, you've bin jailed enough. But Uncle Jeff ain't here. And when he gits here, you won't be in any kind of shape to hear what he has to say. We ketched you red-handed and hung you, you

45

damned horse thief, to the first tree."

And only because there was no tree within a fifty-mile distance, Galt and Hipshot lived to see another sunrise. They camped for a few hours the next day because every man of the Mill Iron was dead tired for sleep. They had been in the saddle continuously for two days and nights, trailing the stolen horses, and they had to have rest.

At that, Lon Coulter might have shot Galt and Hipshot. But the older hands would not have it. They half believed Hipshot's story that he and Galt had taken the stolen horses away from Pecos Moss. Only Lon Coulter and two others were profanely emphatic in their scoffing.

"Three men run off part of our remuda," snarled Lon. "It's my guess that Pecos Moss was with you two. He got away when we corralled you. This talk against Pecos Moss ain't gittin' acrost with me, Hipshot. You're a damned, whiskey guzzlin', lyin' thief. And coward enough to try to crawl and whine out of it. You and this button pardner of yourn. You ain't gettin' away with it. You killed the nighthawk and run off seventy-five head of top horses. We should reach the Canadian by sundown. There's trees along the Canadian."

A few hours later they were again in the

saddle. As Lon Coulter tied Hipshot's galled wrists to the saddle horn, the range tramp grinned faintly and nodded towards the skyline.

"Injuns, Lon. A good-sized war party, or I'm a pilgrim. We'll be damned lucky if any of us ever live to see them cottonwoods on the Canadian River. When a war party gits this far away from their stompin' grounds, they ain't out fer the fun of it. And they'd ruther have these horses than all the cattle that ever went up the trail. When they attack, you'd better give me and Galt our guns. You'll need us."

Lon Coulter did not reply. It was his first trip up the trail and Jeff Curtis had left him in charge of the outfit while he went to Las Vegas. The sight of those Indians riding along the skyline for a few minutes, then vanishing as if by magic, worried him. Hipshot saw the puzzled look in his eyes as the Indians vanished from sight as suddenly as they had appeared. He followed his advantage.

"Me and Galt knowed we was sighted before you found us. You showin' up unexpected kep' them red devils from attackin' me and my pardner. The Injuns made their smoke signals and other Injuns sighted the smoke and whipped their ponies down the hind laig. Now that they figger there's enough of 'em to wipe us out, they'll attack as soon as dark comes. Or mebby before dark, if there's enough of 'em. If you'd treated me and my pardner like white men, I'd have warned you before to send for help. Now you're in a tight and there ain't a seasoned Injun fighter amongst yuh. I'm the only man here that's ever had personal dealin's with Injun war parties. I'm tellin' you, mister, you're in a tight. You just finished callin' me a damned liar. You'll find out before you're many hours older that I'm not lyin' when I say you're in an almighty tight fix. Now tie me to the saddle horn if you think it'll help your odds."

Lon Coulter scowled as he knotted the rope around the saddle horn. He got on his horse and rode off to get the horses started. Leaving Hipshot and Galt with the two men whose job it was to lead the horses of the prisoners.

"When them Injuns pull the tail feathers from that rooster," grinned Hipshot, "he won't be crowin' no more."

"If we was to untie you and your pardner, Hipshot," said one of the Mill Iron men, "and give you your guns, what would you do, first thing?"

"I'd be sore tempted to shoot a few holes

through Lon Coulter," admitted the range tramp, "but my better judgment would tell me that every white man in this outfit would be needed if we ever hope to make the Canadian and reinforcements. There's about a hundred of them Injuns."

The cowboy nodded, turning to the man who held the bridle reins of Galt's horse.

"Lon's bin actin' like a damn' fool. Me, I've claimed right along that Hipshot has bin tellin' a straight story. I'm seein' the rest of the boys and if they're agreeable Hipshot and his pardner git their guns back. And that ain't all. I'm plumb in favor of Hipshot givin' orders to the rest of us, Lon Coulter included, from here on. Lon's as bewildered as a mammyless calf at a round-up. We need an old, tough hand if we expect to come through alive." Handing Hipshot's bridle reins to his companion, he spurred away to join the other cowhands.

Galt and Hipshot saw the Texans talking among themselves. Saw Lon Coulter join them. For some minutes a heated argument went on. Then the man who had left the prisoners rode back. He had the two saddle guns and six-shooters belonging to the prisoners. There was a faint, grim smile on his bearded lips.

"Lon's fit to be tied," he said, as he cut

Hipshot and Galt free and gave them their guns, "but he was out-voted aplenty. And if we was to know the truth, I bet he's willin' enough, down inside his heart, to turn over the ramrod job to an old hand. Hipshot, give the orders. We'll take 'em. Regardless."

"Look your guns over careful, Galt," said Hipshot. "I wouldn't put it past the whelp of Joe Coulter to monkey with our shootin' irons. He's got eyes and a tongue like Joe had. And Joe's ways were treacherous."

Then the range tramp who had been called a thief, a coward, a whiskey-guzzling liar and other hard names, took charge of the men and horses. He gave orders in a flat, grim tone that made men obey without question. His blue eyes were hard as glass.

"Galt, cut the packs off our two pack hosses. We're travelin' light from here on. And listen, every man of yuh. Our one chance is to git to the Mill Iron camp before night. String the horses out at a long trot. Don't let 'em slow up unless I say so. And don't crowd 'em faster than a road trot. When the horse under you starts gittin' the least bit laig weary, dab your line on a fresh 'un and change. And don't drop too far behind while you're saddlin' your fresh horse. Because we ain't got time to wait for yuh. If them Injuns try to cut us off, make every

50

shot count. Don't waste lead. Keep your heads cool. And keep these ponies on the move. The only kind of a fight we kin make is a runnin' fight. That's all."

Galt cut the beds and light camp outfit from the two pack horses. Taking only a few things from his warsack. He took the blood-stained, buckskin-covered Bible and shoved it into the bosom of his heavy flannel shirt.

Hipshot, getting tobacco and extra cartridges from his own warsack, nodded as Galt stowed away his father's Bible.

"Preacher Sam," he said, "would like that, son. . . ."

Now and then, to the right and left, sometimes ahead, showed small groups of Indians riding. They would top a ridge or a knoll, then disappear again. Always in small bunches of a dozen or so. Never showing themselves for more than a few minutes. On either side, beyond gunshot range. Flanking the white men who kept the horses moving at a long trot.

Hour after hour. It was mid-afternoon and the sun was hot. No water. There would be no water until they reached the Canadian. And though the Indians still showed at intervals, they had made no move to attack. Lon Coulter rode up on the point. Not once had he come within earshot of Galt or Hipshot. Especially Hipshot. He and one of the two men who had voted against letting the prisoners have their guns, rode together. And as the chances of an Indian attack seemed more and more remote, Lon began to regain his self-confidence. And he was galling under the humiliation of having Hipshot give orders to the Mill Iron cowboys.

Hipshot rode back with Galt, mostly, bringing up the drags, saying little, his restless, puckered blue eyes scanning the skyline, watching the Indians, who showed now and then for brief minutes. Using his field glasses. Passing remarks to Galt. Paying hardly any attention to the men who were following out his orders.

Now and then Lon Coulter, riding up on the point, called some remark across the moving horses to the men on the opposite point.

"Ain't more than a dozen Injuns trailin' us!" Galt heard him call to the cowpunchers on the other point. His voice carried back with the wind, and he seemed to want his remarks heard, for his voice was louder than necessary.

"Some scare you let that range tramp throw into you," he went on. "There ain't enough Injuns this near the Canadian to make a war whoop sound like more than coyotes yappin'. You let him scare you into givin' him his guns. I told you he was runnin' a whizzer with his Injun talk."

Hipshot looked sideways at Galt and grinned, though his blue eyes were narrowed and dangerous.

"Don't let Lon Coulter git advantage of you in any way, son. He's on the prod. That's trouble talk he's a-makin'. He's keepin' that gent with him in case he needs him to back a gunplay. Though he won't go fer his gun unless the odds are all on his side. I knowed his daddy. Joe Coulter fit thataway. No matter what happens, you stick close by me. And them dozen Injuns will tally close to a hundred. I bin watchin'. Near as I kin make out, no bunch shows twice. It's a new bunch every time that tops the skyline. If Lon knowed that, his shirt would git itchy along his backbone where the yaller runs wide along his spine. Them Injuns is sorta sizin' us up. And when the sign is right, they'll have at us."

Because Hipshot made no attempt to deny the taunts Lon Coulter was calling across to the other cowhands, the disgruntled young ramrod of the Mill Iron was getting bolder. It was almost fight talk he was making. It was as if his unchallenged talk was a truth that Hipshot had not the nerve to deny. Moreover, Lon believed what he said about the Indians. That there was no real danger. He and the cowboy siding him roped a fresh mount apiece and led them off to one side about fifty yards to change. Letting the other cowpunchers go past with the horses.

In defiant disobedience of Hipshot's orders not to waste time changing horses, Lon and the cowboy were taking their time. They turned loose their sweaty horses and leisurely saddled the fresh mounts. Until they were almost half a mile behind when they finally mounted.

And as if that were a signal, the Indians attacked. Coming from all sides with a rush. It was as if every bush and rock on the hills had concealed an Indian on horseback. They came, yelling, shooting, swinging in a circle to surround the white men and the horses they were after.

Hipshot swore through set teeth. Then he shouted orders as he raked his horse with the spurs.

"Turn the horses back! Swing 'em back. Keep 'em close bunched and ride low in the saddle. Keep close to the horses, boys! They don't want to hit the horses and they're shootin' high. They're shootin' to stampede 'em. Keep them ponies bunched. Coulter

54

and that other man is back yonder. Our only chance to save the two damn' fools is to move back to 'em. Damn their fool hides. Ride low along your horses' necks, cowboys. And close to the cavvy. Keep the ponies bunched. Make your shots count. Haze 'em back to Coulter and his fool pardner. . . ."

And then, as the Texans bunched the frightened horses and got them started back, the fight was on.

Old Hipshot knew Indians and their ways. Knew that they would not risk killing or crippling the horses they were after. That they were making a try at stampeding the stock and killing the cowboys later, when danger of hitting the horses with bullets and arrows was over.

It called upon every bit of skill and nerve the Texans had to hold together the cavvy of terrified horses. By sheer luck they got them headed back towards where Lon Coulter and the other cowboy were trapped in a buffalo wallow, cut off from their outfit by the wild riding Indians.

Lon Coulter was no coward, for all his treacherous ways. And he did not lose his wits. The only chance he and his partner had was to quit their horses and lay flat on their bellies in the meager shelter of the buffalo wallow.

They jerked their saddle guns as they dismounted. And each of them unbuckled his rope.

"Tie your rope to the end of your bridle reins," gritted Lon, "and hang onto the other end. So's our horses can't quit us. Our one bet is to make a stand. Kill as many as we can till they finish us. While they git a meal, we'll take a few nibbles. We'll — damn!"

A bullet had struck Lon's horse in the head. The animal leaped forward, then turned over and lay on its side. A few convulsive kicks and it was dead.

Bullets were snarling all around. Lon dropped behind the dead horse, taking a snapshot at the nearest Indian racing past. His shot was lucky. The Indian, shot through the head, tumbled from the back of his painted pony. Lon turned his head to say something to his partner. The words stuck in his throat. The man lay on his back, eyes staring, blood oozing from his open mouth. Dead.

Lon pulled the dear man closer and used the body to shield his own. And his next shot toppled an Indian from the back of his running horse. The horse of the dead Texan had run off, dragging the rope tied to the bridle reins. Lou Coulter was afoot. And

56

while the majority of the Indians were engaged in the main attack, about ten or a dozen were trying to kill Lon as they raced past, lying on the far side of their horses, shooting from under the necks of their mounts.

Most of the shots were going wild. A few came too close for comfort. Lon lay on his belly behind the dead horse and the dead body of his partner. And tried to make his bullets count.

If the Texan was afraid to die, he gave no sign of that fear. His black eyes were reddish slits in the sunset, his face grim, gray, jaws clamped. His hands were steady. His aim true.

It was a fool thing to do. A fool thing, and a desperately brave thing. And Galt himself never knew why he did it. He owed nothing to Lon Coulter.

But there was the chance, that chance against odds he never even figured. A gap in the circle of painted Indians. And not a hundred yards beyond, Lon cut off from the white men, putting up a lone, grim fight. Galt raked his horse with spurs. He lay low along the neck of his running horse. If he was being shot at, he didn't know it. His own six-shooter was in his hand. But no Indian tried to cut him off. Perhaps they thought he was suddenly crazy. Or it might have been that they were too shocked by surprise to shoot at him or try to cut him off from the lone fighter in the buffalo wallow.

Lon had shot four of the Indians who had been circling him. The others had ridden off a distance. Lon saw Galt racing towards him. And as Galt slid his horse to a halt and held out an arm, Lon grabbed it and vaulted on back of him. And hardly before the shod hoofs had slid to a halt, they were pounding again on the run.

Only when the horse with its double burden was through the broken circle of Indians did any man, white or red, fully realize what Galt had done.

The horse that had belonged to the dead Texan was back with the cavvy. Someone caught the dragging rope and led the horse at a lope to Lon who slid from behind Galt and into the empty saddle. There was a smear of blood on his gray face that came from a bullet wound across his cheek. He had a queer sort of grin on his mouth as he looked at Galt. As Galt whirled his horse and joined Hipshot, who was cursing him in a harsh, choked voice.

"Of all the thick-headed, half-witted things I ever seen! And I used to call Preacher Sam loco. . . . You come by it natural! Bunch them ponies, boys! Swing 'em back! And the next man that acts the damn fool gits left behind! Shoot a gap through them Injuns and push these ponies through. We got 'em licked! They're a-scatterin'! Push them ponies through! We got them sons of britch-clout, moccasin-hoofed heathen on the run. Give 'em hell!"

The Indians were scattering, heading back for the hills. And the Texans with their horse cavvy were under way. Then the cause of this unexpected easy victory showed itself. Riders coming over the hills from the direction of the Canadian River. A score or more of hard-riding cowpunchers, coming on a run.

The fighting was over. The rescue party, men from the Mill Iron and another trail herd, rode up. They had gotten news from a plainsman scout that there was a big war party riding and had set out to protect Lon Coulter and his men who had chased the horse thieves.

And as the sun set, a grave was dug in the buffalo wallow and the only Texan who had been killed, was buried there. And at Hipshot's insistence, Galt Magrath got out the bloodstained, buckskin-covered old Bible that had belonged to his father, and read from it. Read a passage from a dog-eared, thumb-marked page.

It was Hipshot who had found the right passage. "I've seen Preacher Sam read this here page many a time, at plantin's."

"The Lord giveth . . . taketh away."

While the cowpunchers stood there in the dusk, bareheaded. And Galt's voice sounded through a strange hush.

Then the grave was filled and the place hidden by the tracks of horses that were driven across it. And they rode on with the horses to the Mill Iron camp on the Canadian.

Hipshot and Galt rode together behind the drags. The moon came up and they recognized Lon Coulter as he came riding towards them from up on the point of the horses they still moved at a pace that was faster than a walk. Hipshot's hand dropped to his gun. Lon had two men with him. He looked at Galt with a faint, humorless grin.

"Don't think I'm goin' to slobber all over you with thanks for savin' my hide. I didn't holler for help. Even your pardner Hipshot cussed you out for it.

"What you did back yonder when you made a tin hero out of yourself don't in ary way change my opinion of you and Hipshot. You're still a pair of horse thieves to me.

"But you've put me in your debt. So I'm

payin' off that debt. There won't be ary hangin'. When we reach camp, you're welcome to fill your bellies. Then pull out. And don't cut my sign again unless you come a-shootin'. That pays you two off. Understand?"

"Perfect," said Hipshot.

Lon Coulter and the two men with him rode on. Hipshot grinned twistedly.

"Don't look like we'll be goin' up the trail with the Mill Iron herd, son. Even when Jeff Curtis shows up and hears our side of it, and believes our story, and even if he stuck to his promise to hire us, we couldn't go. Jeff and Lon Coulter is kinfolks and blood is thicker than water. There'd be janglin' and trouble. And so I reckon we'll go on to Dodge City. There'll be other trail herds goin' to Montana. We'll hire out to one of 'em. Though I'd ruther work for Jeff Curtis than ary man I know. But hoss thieves can't be choosers. I'm a dawg with a bad name. I reckon you've kinda suspicioned that, by now. And you're wise enough now to know the ropes. You'll be a heap better off goin' alone. Trailin' with a renegade like me ain't —"

"Say, did you get holt of a bottle somewhere, you damned ol' hipshot idiot? You talk drunk and loco. We'll go up the trail together or not at all." Galt's tone was genuinely wrathful.

"All right, all right. Tuck in your shirt tail." A smile softened the weatherbeaten face of the range tramp and his blue eyes were bright as stars under the brim of his battered hat.

"You know, son," he said, as they rode along behind the horses, "back yonder, when you read from that old Bible, in the twilight, your voice sounded for all the world like Preacher Sam's. And when you stood there, tall and straight, and your head tilted, you looked a lot like Sam did years ago. Before ever you was born. When he was a wanderin' young sky-pilot and the Bible you got now was new. Before he got married.

"I seen Sam Magrath once hand his Bible to a bartender to hold safe fore him. While he took off his black coat and rolled back his sleeves and whipped half a dozen men. . . . Sam Magrath was a man. In lots of ways, you're the spittin' image of him."

For a moment Galt thought that Hipshot was going to tell him something about his father. He knew that the grizzled old range tramp was holding back something that had happened, years ago, that he wanted to talk about, yet always changed his mind at the last moment. Galt knew that his father and Hipshot had been bound by a strong friendship of some sort. It was what Hipshot left unsaid that made Galt the more certain that back in those past years there had been something almighty important that had gone to make for that friendship. But Galt, eaten though he was by curiosity, asked no questions.

"Did Sam ever tell you about your mother, Galt?" Hipshot broke a long silence.

"Nothin' much."

Hipshot nodded. "Treatin' her as he did, son, was the only real wrong Sam Magrath ever did as long as I knowed him. Mary was as fine a woman as ever breathed the breath of life. . . ."

And though Galt waited with all the patience he could summon to keep his tongue still, old Hipshot did not break the silence that followed. Nor did Galt dare to say a word.

And at daybreak they sighted the Canadian. As their horses drank, Hipshot nodded towards the giant cottonwoods on the bank.

"My favor-ite tree. If I had to be hung, I'd ruther it'd be from a cottonwood instead of a sycamore er piñon er hackberry er blackjack."

63

IV

A week later Hipshot and Galt were in Dodge City. They had not lingered back on the Canadian for the coming of Jeff Curtis. The Mill Iron camp was too small to hold Hipshot and Lon Coulter without gunpowder being burned.

They had money in their pockets and time on their hands. And the metropolis of the cattle trail inviting them to enjoy its wide open brand of hospitality.

They had hardly stabled their horses before Hipshot had met men he knew. For he had been up the trail three times and had traveled over every mile of the southwest cattle country. He had made many friends and a few enemies. And he walked warily always when in town.

Though Galt said nothing about it to Hipshot, he had his own personal reasons for remembering Dodge. It was here that he had been taken by his mother, when he was a small boy of about six. His memory of it all was dim. He recognized none of the buildings of this mushroom cow town. The years had spread it out, changed things. And there was nothing familiar about its dusty streets, its rows of frame buildings, mostly saloons and gambling houses, with their high, false fronts and their wooden awnings across wide plank sidewalks. But as he and Hipshot stabled their horses and walked down the street, Galt's eyes kept searching for the hotel where he had stopped with his mother. And dim, half forgotten memories crowded like half formed shadows in his mind. Like ghosts walking. And the only clear picture that showed through the shadows was that of his mother. A beautiful, tear-stained face, ivory-white, more beautiful for her suffering, crowned by a mass of copper-colored hair. Large, gray eyes with long, thick black lashes.

Inside Galt was an aching, burning pain that weighted his heart. And because Hipshot would not notice his silence, his lack of interest in the sporting fun Dodge offered, he almost hated the old range tramp. Old Hipshot must know the story of Mary

Magrath's flight to Dodge with her small son. How Preacher Sam had followed and overtaken them there. And how he had taken her child from her and left her alone here in this wild frontier town. Then why didn't Hipshot say something? Why didn't he talk? Talk about something besides whiskey and gambling and dance-hall gals? Damn it all, why didn't he quit being so mysterious?

It was getting dark and the lights were coming on. Galt halted in front of a building that bore a sun-cracked sign **HOTEL**. Frowning, he studied it. This might be the place. It had been run by a man and his wife. Galt remembered the man was fat and bald and had a big red mustache and a bulbous purplish nose. The woman had been a flat-chested, sharp featured, rasping-tongued slattern. Galt had hated her and that child-hood hatred had kept a sort of picture of the woman in his mind's eye.

There was a saloon and eating place downstairs off the office with its pine-board desk and a cowbell on a string that you sounded to call the proprietor from the bar or his shrewish wife from the kitchen. Galt stepped inside, trying to remember the sur-roundings. They seemed vaguely familiar. Yes, there was the cowbell hanging by its

66

rawhide string. An inkstand alongside a ledger used as a register. A pen stuck in a half potato. A board on which were numbers and the room keys fastened to numbered wooden paddles hung there. A huge brass cuspidor.

Galt's heart was pounding now like a triphammer. He took hold of the cowbell and rang it noisily. And for the first time he took notice that Hipshot had followed him in and was standing there, weight slouched on one long leg, standing "hipshot," thumbs hooked in the sagging cartridge belt that hung somehow to his hipless flanks. There was a queer look on his weatherbeaten face as he watched Galt.

No aproned, paunchy, mustached man came from the bar that was crowded. No slattern with hair pulled back in a biscuit knot on top of her head came from the dining-room beyond. It was suppertime and it was as crowded as the saloon. Galt scowled faintly, and was about to say something to Hipshot, who had watched and waited wordlessly when a girl came down the narrow stairs that led to the rooms above. As Galt stared, awed, awkward, at the first white woman he had seen in weeks — for his brief stay in Las Vegas had been devoid of any sight of women — the girl descended the stairs and spoke directly to him.

"You rang the bell?"

She had eyes as dark blue as a sky he had seen one evening in New Mexico just at dusk when the evening star showed over the mountains. And thick, black, wavy hair with strange blue highlights that showed under the big hanging lamp. Her skin was tanned, red-cheeked, glowing with health. Her lips as red as a berry before the frost. Strong, even, white teeth. And her voice was low-pitched, soft. The sort of a voice that a green bronc savvies and wild animals hear without scaring. But the sound of it almost made Galt jump.

The girl, she was about Galt's age, must have realized something of his embarrassment, for she went right on talking as she walked in behind the shabby desk.

"It's suppertime and they're too busy to answer the bell, even if they heard it in the saloon or diningroom. There's only the Snake Room left and you won't want that. It's the room above the saloon and when the cowboys commence shooting up through the ceiling, it's dangerous to be sleeping, or trying to sleep, up above. They call it the snake room because it's where they put drunks and occasional corpses. Men that get shot downstairs, you know, or out in the street. Dodge brags about its thriving boot-hill." And when she laughed, Galt's embarrassment lessened some, though there were beads of sweat on his forehead as he hauled off his dusty hat.

And it added none to his peace of mind to suddenly realize that he was dusty and sweaty and that his clothes were dirty and ragged and a little spattered with old blood, and that there was a boyish growth of beard on his face and his hair was long and matted with sweat and dust against his head. He stood there, dumb. And he thanked God for the welcome sound of old Hipshot's voice.

"You've grown a lot and filled out here and there and you ain't barelegged and wearin' cotton britches and a man's shirt, and you've got your hair fixed and you're dressed like a growed-up lady. But I'll go to jail fer a liar if you ain't little Nancy Curtis from down on the San Saba."

"Hipshot!" And she was around the counter and had thrown her arms around the disreputable-looking old rascal who looked and acted almighty pleased. And his eyes, looking over her head, were twinkling merrily as he grinned at the gaping Galt.

Nancy Curtis was the only daughter of Jeff Curtis. Her mother had died when she was five years old and a colored mammy, Aunt Cloe, had raised her at San Saba. All this and many other things about her, Galt was to learn later.

"Nan, shake hands with my young pardner, Galt Magrath. His daddy was Preacher Sam, that baptized you and preached the sermon at your mother's funeral. Galt ain't as dumb as he looks right now. You just nacherally scared hell outa him, that's all. Showin' up like a mornin' glory — Galt, pull the slack up on your jaw and meet Nancy Curtis, Jeff's young 'un. What in tarnation you doin' at Dodge?" he asked her.

"Waiting for dad and the trail herd. Didn't you come up with the Mill Iron herd?"

"Not exactly," chuckled Hipshot. "But we seen Jeff at Las Vegas. He looked fat an' sassy as ever. Chipper as a medderlark. Me and Galt was in a sort of hurry so we come on ahead."

"You're going with the Mill Iron cattle when they're shipped?" Nan Curtis asked a question but seemed to take the answer for granted.

"Before I left home I heard dad say he wanted to take along only men he could depend on. And that he'd heard you'd got religion and quit wandering and he hoped he could find you and take you with us to Montana. Of course he told you that we'd sold our ranch on the San Saba and bought this bunch of Mill Iron cattle and a bunch of top horses and we're goin' into business for ourselves, dad and me, in Montana. I came by wagon train with Aunt Cloe. Got here ten days ago. They kill a man for breakfast every morning. What's holding back the trail herd? Hipshot are you holding back anything? Has anything happened?"

"The trail herd is comin' along, as quick as Jeff ketches up. They laid over on the Canadian to put a little taller on the cattle while Jeff tended to some business at Las Vegas." His grin became a chuckle.

"By the color of Galt's face, I wouldn't be su'prised if he'd kinda like to have his gun hand back when you git done holdin' onto it."

"Oh!" Nancy let go Galt's hand like it had suddenly turned into a hot branding iron. She had been so excited at seeing Hipshot and getting news of her father that she'd been clinging to Galt's hand as she talked to Hipshot. And now, for the first time, she really seemed to look at the young cowpuncher. Her face was crimson. She and Galt, both red with embarrassment, looked at one another. Then they suddenly laughed. And the formality between them was forever broken.

A short, fat, shining black Negress appeared at the head of the stairs.

"Lawzy, Honey!" she called down. "You like to scared me pale yaller. Runnin' off thataway. This here hell hole of wickedness ain't fittin fo' nuthin' but misery. Honey, chile, iffen you-all don' want to kill yo' Aunt Cloe wid heart failin's, stay up in yo' room an' quit minglin' wid po' white trash — Lawdy if it ain't 'at shif'less, no-count, pie-stealin' Hipshot. Wha' at is Mista Jeff Curtis?"

"I left him plumb surrounded by Injuns and five hundred Mexicans. He was gittin' low on ca'tridges and hadn't et grub ner drank water in thirteen days. And it wasn't me that stole your pie, that evenin' at the ranch. It was — it was Nancy. Only bein' a gentleman, I taken the blame fer a lady."

"We have a sitting-room upstairs," said Nancy. "We'd better go up there and talk."

"Later," said Hipshot. "Me'n Galt has some business to 'tend to. Such as gittin' a hair trim and a bath and clean duds. You better git back upstairs before Aunt Cloe fetches you by an ear."

The girl nodded. "Come up later, then.

Aunt Cloe don't let me come downstairs. I'm anxious about dad. Worried. Since what happened to my Uncle Frank —"

"Shucks, young 'un, Jeff's plumb safe."

"Why did he go to Las Vegas? It's clear off the trail. He hadn't planned going there when he left the home ranch. Did it have anything to do with what happened to Frank?"

"He didn't say. I didn't git a chance to chin much with him. But he had four-five of the Mill Iron boys with him, so he's safe enough. You trot upstairs, before that black thunder-cloud up yonder busts."

When she had gone, Hipshot's grin faded. "Her uncle started up the trail with that San Saba Pool herd. Never was heard of since. Frank was a wild devil and put many a gray hair in Jeff's head, with his gamblin' and hell raisin'. But he wasn't as onery as Lon Coulter and the others he trailed with. A man couldn't help but like Frank Curtis."

"Was he among the dead gents buried, there where the wagons got burned and the outfit wiped out?"

It was a direct question and Hipshot had half expected it. And while his answer was plausible enough, Galt felt that the old range tramp was protecting the missing Frank Curtis with an evasive answer.

"I told you they'd bin dead some time when I found 'em. The buzzards and coyotes had scattered their bones. Some of 'em had bin burned. So a man couldn't tell fer positive who the dead was or who got away."

And Galt didn't remind him of the remark he'd made the day he led him to the spot of the wholesale massacre of the San Saba Pool outfit. Hipshot had said then that he'd know the ones that got away, when he cut their sign. The two men Hipshot had killed back at Las Vegas, Little Jack and The Cuter, had been mixed up in the massacre. So had Pecos Moss. Hipshot had told Galt that much. He'd never mentioned the name of Frank Curtis in connection with the rustlers. And he wondered now about the strange look that had passed between Jeff Curtis and Hipshot in the restaurant that night in Las Vegas.

Hipshot walked behind the counter and took a key from the board. Unlike the other paddles, the one attached to this room key was painted. Green with yellow spots on one side. Black on the other. And some jack-knife artist had fashioned it in the shape of a coffin. It had no number.

"Looks like me'n you git the bridal chamber," said Hipshot. "We'll buy some blankets and spread 'em in the Snake

Room. It ain't as bad as Nancy tells it. Like as not somebody's bin throwin' a load into her. This ain't the hotel that was here some years ago. The old 'un burned down. The couple that run it burned with it, and a good riddance. This 'un was built a few years ago. These cow-town hotels all look about alike." Hipshot indicated the adjoining saloon and dining-room.

"You was hopin' to find trace of your mother, Galt?" he asked in a low tone.

"Yes. I was hopin' you'd help me."

"You won't find track of her here, son. I'm hopin' we'll be able to hear of her in Montana. She went north from here. Changed her name and plumb disappeared. God knows I tried hard enough to pick up her trail. She ain't nowhere in the Southwest. I've bin over every mile of it. And twice up the trail to Montana. Nary sign of Mary Galt that become Mary Magrath when she married Preacher Sam. Mebbyso she's dead. But you'll only be wastin' time huntin' trace of her in Dodge. So let's go buy some clean duds and a bath and a haircut and shave. And while I trim these tinhorn gamblers and wash the dust outa my throat, you kin set in Nancy's parlor and git acquainted. Her being mammyless, like you, the two of you should git along fine.

But you'll want to git shut of them rags and dirt. Come along."

"She's worried about her father."

"Yeah. And she's got me worryin' some. I'll smell around fer news. Jeff owin' them Mill Iron cattle and about two hundred head of horses puts a new color on things. I'm wonderin' if Jeff or Nancy told anybody about Jeff ownin' them cattle? Because it'd make a hell of a lot of difference to rustlers like Pecos Moss. They'd raid a herd owned by a single owner like Jeff Curtis. Where they'd be scared to monkey with a herd belongin' to a big outfit like the Mill Iron that'd foller 'em to hell and kill 'em. And Jeff was keepin' it a secret or he'd have told me back at Las Vegas that he owned the trail herd. Mind, I said somethin' about the Mill Iron when I made you acquainted with him. And he never denied he was still workin' fer the outfit and lettin' Nancy take care of his own little spread. Jeff wasn't tellin' nobody he was on his own. Because he knowed the risk he'd be runnin' as an individual owner. He wasn't forgittin' what happened to the little owners of the San Saba Pool. There wasn't none of them left to track down the rustlers and claim the stolen cattle. And there'd be nobody left to go gunnin' fer the rustlers that killed off Jeff Curtis and stole his cattle. The Mill Iron sold them cattle to Jeff. They was all branded with a road iron. A Lazy J on the right ribs. The Mill Iron is a big spread. Too busy to take up a dead man's grudge. Who'd be left to trail down the rustlers that killed Jeff Curtis and stole his cattle? Nobody but that treacherous snake Lon Coulter who might be in with 'em from the start. And a sixteen-year-old girl."

"You're forgettin' Frank Curtis, ain't you?"

"I'm countin' Frank dead, son. There's no other way to tally him." Hipshot's eyes were hard, puckered.

"Git cleaned up, Galt," he said, as they halted in front of a general store, "and ride herd on Nancy. I'm goin' to smell around some. And I'm puttin' off my drunk till I find out a few things. And be where I kin locate you if I need yuh. Hold down Nancy's second-best chair in the hotel parlor. And don't let on like we're worried about Jeff. But be ready to hightail it out of Dodge if need be."

Hipshot almost shoved Galt into the store, then went on to the nearest saloon.

Galt bought a new outfit of clothes and headed for the barber shop. Passing a saloon he saw Hipshot talking to a man at the end of the bar. The man had been pointed out by Hipshot when they had ridden into town. The man was the famous frontier peace officer of Dodge City, Bat Masterson.

In the three years or more that Galt had trailed with Hipshot, he had grown to view law officers with a somewhat jaundiced eye. A law badge was liable to mean complications. For old Hipshot was undoubtedly kin to the proverbial dog with a bad name. And from the expression on his seamed, humorous, unshaven face, and the stern look on the face of Dodge's famous Marshal, Galt read trouble. He looked around for a place to hide his bundle. But there seemed to be no suitable hiding place handy. The barber shop was next door. He took it there.

"Keep this till I come in. It's clean clothes. I'll be wantin' a haircut and shave and a hot bath before you close." And he shoved the big bundle on a shelf beneath a smaller shelf that held a row of privately owned shaving mugs and brushes. One ornate mug bore the name of Bat Masterson in gilt letters.

Rid of his bundle that might be cumbersome in case of a fight, Galt slipped into the crowded saloon as unobtrusively as possible. To take his stand near the door. He maneuvered to keep Bat Masterson's back towards him. And did his best to catch Hipshot's eye.

Hipshot was talking earnestly, a filled glass in his hand. Bat Masterson was listening. Galt, nervous as he was, could not help admiring the peace officer. He was the boy's ideal of a law officer. Handsome and quietly dressed in town clothes, without swagger or bluster in his manner. This was the man who was making Dodge a town fit to live in. He was doing a tremendous job.

It took a real man to wear the badge pinned to Bat Masterson's vest. With the aid of such fearless deputies as Wyatt Earp, Bill Tilghman, Chalk Beeson, Luke Short and other decent-minded citizens, he was making it hard on outlaws and hoodlums who had given Dodge the name of being the toughest cow town in the West.

To Galt, this peace officer, with his fearlessness, his quiet ways, his decent standards, stood for ideals that Preacher Sam had talked about in his fiery sermons. And Galt felt a little ashamed of old Hipshot who was a rascal and a range tramp and with no claim to honesty and virtue. And then almost in the same instant he hated himself for that disloyalty to old Hipshot who was his pardner. . . . If it came to a tight, he'd face all the law on earth to fight at the side of the grizzled range tramp. Galt's hand slid along the cedar butt of his gun and he edged a little closer.

Then Hipshot caught sight of him, over Bat Masterson's wide shoulder. And his keen blue eyes missed nothing of the young cowboy's intentions. His lips twitched in a smile that softened the hard lines of his face. He said something to Bat Masterson in low-pitched tone. Bat Masterson turned around. And Galt found himself looking squarely into the law officer's eyes. Bat Masterson smiled faintly and said something to Hipshot.

"Come here, son," called Hipshot, "and shake the hand of a real man. I was tellin' Bat about you when I sighted you, crouched fer all the world like a cougar about to jump." He chuckled deep in his throat.

Galt was hot with embarrassment. But inside his heart was a feeling that a hard, aching lump had suddenly dissolved. Hipshot seemed to sort of understand, for he all but voiced Galt's thoughts when he spoke.

"After that Las Vegas deal, Bat, the button was commencin' to think he was a-trailin' with a shore enough bad aig. And with ropes agittin' tight around our necks, you might say, he was losin' his respect fer his pardner. Hot as the sun was and bad as we needed shade, we was shore glad there wasn't no trees around when Lon Coulter was makin' his talk. Galt, I know a few men on this earth that are not rustlers and ornery. Bat Masterson's one. Pattern your ways after his and you won't be far from the teachin's of your daddy. Preacher Sam used a Bible to put the fear of Gawd into the sinners. Bat's tools is his guns."

"I knew your father," said Bat Masterson, and the way he said it quickened Galt's pulse. Afterwards he remembered it as being about the finest compliment he had ever heard paid Preacher Sam.

"If I need you, son," said Hipshot, "I'll find you at the hotel. Git cleaned up and ride close herd on little Nancy. While me and Bat kinda listen to what the breeze whispers. And you don't need to cold trail me. I ain't raisin' ary hell. And you kin see for yourself I'm travelin' in society. Now git purtied-up. If Aunt Cloe gits snuffy, pull the Bible on her and she'll be your friend for life. You might try and locate that there part that speaks of the fattened calf. Only sort of twist the meanin' into terms of fried chicken. And hint around that there's wrinkles a inch deep in your belly from hunger. And if she takes the hint and kin locate the fowl, and if she falls hard fer your Bible preachin', you'll be tastin' the finest fried chicken you ever throwed a lip over. Her and Preacher Sam used to git along somethin' grand. Now lope along. Me and Bat is makin' medicine."

Galt was excited as a small boy with his first pair of brass-toed, red-topped boots as he went into the barber shop. He had shaken hands with Dodge City's famous Bat Masterson. He was basking in the light of its glory. And it took him almost a full minute to realize that his bundle of clothes was not there on the shelf. And the barber, with a lack of memory that was startling, disclaimed any knowledge of having even seen it. Though it had been in plain sight, almost in his way as he worked. The several men in the shop were getting no little enjoyment out of the young cowboy's bewilderment.

"I put it here on the shelf and said I'd be back for it. I told you I'd want a bath and haircut and shave. I was only gone a few minutes. Mebby you put it away somewheres."

"Young feller, I'm too busy to look after stray bundles. What did you have in it? Rags?" And he looked Galt up and down with a tipsy eye and a jeering grin. One of the men in the place laughed.

Galt's face went hot. The barber was a

man with red sleeve bands that had been the garters of some light o' love. His mustaches were waxed to needle points and his hair sleeked down with perfumed hair oil. His soft, white hands stropped his razor. With his fancy vest, coatless, a big, gold chain and ornate watch charm, his striped pants and shiny, pointed shoes, he fancied himself quite a dude. And a town cut-up, by his manner.

The range-bred Galt smarted under the ridicule of the town sport. He stood there, his face reddening, then losing its color, as the barber made two or three smart Aleck remarks at the cowboy's expense.

The men sitting around laughed. The barber laid his razor down to reach for the lather-filled mug and brush to lather the customer in the tilted barber-chair.

Galt moved so swiftly that no man there could anticipate his actions. He grabbed the barber by the vest, jerked him around, and with his open hand, swung a short, smacking blow across the man's face. Then, with a calmness and precision that would have done credit to a seasoned rough and tumble fighter, he gave the barber a threshing. And as fast as he knocked the man down, he picked him up, slapped him erect, then flattened him again. The man's nose was spurting blood. One of his eyes was closing rapidly. The other eye was puffing. Galt yanked the man from the floor by his thick, oily hair and propped him against the wall.

"Now mebby you can remember what you did with my bundle."

"It's — in the cupboard where I keep the towels. Don't hit me no more! I got enough!"

The barber's fancy clothes were torn, blood-smeared, ruined. He was slobbering, spitting blood from a bruised, battered mouth. His puffed, discolored eyes streamed with tears as he sobbed, begging for mercy. And those who had jeered, augmented by a big crowd, were giving Galt bits of ribald, jocular advice about what to do with the town sport of Dodge. And whenever Galt came close enough, they slapped him on the back and wanted to buy him drinks.

Galt had noticed the big barrels along the street, filled with water in case of fire. He picked up the struggling barber and carried him out through the doorway. The cheering crowd made way. And Galt deposited the howling barber head first in the nearest water-filled barrel and walked away. Back into the barber shop. He got his bundle of clothes. There was another barber shop down the street. A joyous crowd escorted him there. And one of the crowd, appointing himself leader, made a little speech.

"This young cowboy, a stranger in our midst, wants the works. He just finished workin' over Sport McAllister, your competitor, so's the Sport's best gal wouldn't recognize him. This visitor to the thriving metrop'lis of Dodge City desires the best. I'd advise you, in the best inter'sts of all concerned, mainly to preserve your personal beauty and to keep your shop from being wrecked, to let the gent now occupying the chair, abdicate without ceremony. Let him finish shaving himself or wear the lather on his face till it dries. Our guest needs attention. And we who witnessed the recent chastening of Sport McAllister will stand all expenses. The best is none too good for our honored visitor. As the Mexican says it, young man, our shop is yours. Enter your tonsorial parlor. Take care of him, barber."

And so Galt and his bundle were ushered into the barber shop. And the crowd passed a bottle while the tall spokesman passed the hat. To collect expenses for Galt's bath and haircut and shave. The works, in brief. And it was more than an hour later when he was let out of the chair, thoroughly barbered, and into the arms of the waiting crowd. And it was with some difficulty, and finally with the assistance of one of Bat Masterson's deputies, that Galt got away from them. The deputy, it seemed, had watched the chastisement of the barber called Sport McAllister. And nothing was lost in the telling of it when he related the incident to Bat Masterson and Hipshot later.

"He knocked the Sport down. Then he taken a buckskin-covered book from inside his shirt and laid it on the shelf alongside the shavin' mugs. And as calm and cool as a man whittlin' a stick, he proceeds to give that mouthy whisker artist the damnedest, sweetest whuppin' I ever see a man git. And when he dumps the Sport head down in the rain barrel, he goes back inside, gits his bundle, and takes the buckskin-covered book off the shelf. And the boys take him down the street, none other than Doc Holliday in the lead, to the other barber shop. And Doc passes the hat and collects enough to buy the damn' shop, let alone treat the cowboy to a shave. First time I ever seen that funeral-faced gamblin' Doc Holliday seem to enjoy fun. He'll carry the story plumb to Wyatt Harp and the boys when he goes back to Tombstone.

"But here's the part of the ruckus that

seemed to hit Doc Holliday hardest. He got a look at that book with the buckskin cover. Hang me for a liar, Bat, it was the Bible!"

Nobody had learned Galt's identity. And throughout the telling of the barber-shop fracas, Galt had been nameless. The deputy had mentioned him as just some cowboy off the trail.

Hipshot looked at the deputy, his blue eyes sparkling. "A buckskin-covered Bible? You're plumb certain?"

"I got Doc Holliday's word for it. Doc wouldn't lie."

"Then it was him, Bat. It was Galt. It was Preacher Sam's boy. That calls fer a drink."

And so it was that while Galt sat up in the private parlor Bat Masterson had had fixed up in the hotel for the daughter of his old friend Jeff Curtis, the name of Galt Magrath, son of Preacher Sam, was spoken of in the bar-rooms of Dodge City. And as such things take peculiar and lasting shape, so this incident was to mark Galt and, after a fashion, have a bearing upon his life. And it may be truthfully surmised that old Hipshot had a hand in the making of it all. For he made a colorful yarn of Galt preaching a funeral sermon back along the cattle trail, when a Texan was killed by Indians and buried.

Galt Magrath, son of Preacher Sam Magrath, was given a name, there in the famous old Beatty and Kelley Saloon. And the name stuck, as such nicknames stick along the frontier. Galt Magrath became Gospel Galt.

V

Because they were both young, because they were both strangers in a strange land, Galt and Nancy found friendship without the aid of long acquaintance. Youth, in its carefree stride, takes the barrier of formality without even pausing or taking a deep breath. Both were ranch reared, and their talk was of horses and cattle and trail herds and wagon trains. With Aunt Cloe adding fruity bits of opinion concerning the trail and the rough men who rode it.

Galt was the son of Preacher Sam, so the colored mammy, as Nancy put it, let him inside the home corral. Aunt Cloe regarded nearly all cowboys as foredoomed to eternal hell fire. She referred to Preacher Sam as "de white pillar o' light a-shinin' in de wilderness." And fetched out a large plate of cookies and doughnuts which she had made herself in the kitchen of the hotel.

The horsehair, upholstered chairs and sofa were uncomfortable. But Galt and Nancy did not seem to notice. They ate Aunt Cloe's doughnuts and cookies and talked. While the buxom Negress, who had found a heavy old rocking-chair, fell asleep.

The front parlor was across the hall from the Snake Room. And at Bat Masterson's orders the hotel proprietor had agreed not to use the Snake Room for sobering up drunks.

"I'll use it for stiffs only, Bat. It's the only quiet place in town to lay out a corpse, proper."

"No wakes," said the Marshal of Dodge.

"Nary a wake, Bat. If the boys wants to hold a wake over a stiff, they'll have to use one of the card-rooms. And no shootin' through the ceilin'. I'll put up a sign. So long as Jeff's daughter is here, I'll keep the Dodge House quiet as a graveyard."

Aunt Cloe was snoring peacefully. Nancy winked at Galt and pointed towards the door that the colored mammy had bolted. Aunt Cloe had a deadly and terrible fear of dead people and the Snake Room across the hall.

Galt and Nancy unbolted the door and slipped out into the hallway, closing the door behind them. Then they opened the door at the end of the hall that led out onto a sort of porch. In reality, it was the wooden awning that covered the broad plank walk in front of the hotel. The proprietor, as a safety measure, had put a stout railing, like a fence, around the porch, to keep those whose footing was wobbly, from dropping off and down onto the street. The platform that served the double purpose of porch and awning, slanted slightly towards the street.

Galt and Nancy stood by the railing. They were in the shadow and from their higher perch commanded a view of the street. Next door was the Beatty and Kelley Saloon. Out in front of the saloon and a short distance up the street was a well, boarded in, box fashion, about waist high. It had a hand windlass that pulled up a large bucket fastened to the end of a rope, and four posts supported a V-shaped roof above it. The well served two purposes. It quenched the thirst of those who were dry. And it was an excellent place to sober fractious drunks by the simple method of looping the well rope under their armpits and lowering them via the windlass into the cold depths below.

Even as Galt and Nancy stood leaning over the railing, the doorway of the saloon belched forth a crowd of jostling men. In their midst was a man who struggled vainly in the strong grip of the crowd. His language was blistering with profanity. Galt took the girl's arm to lead her back inside but Nancy laughed and shook her head.

"I've heard cussing since I was old enough to savvy the Mex and Texas language, Galt. I know most of the words. I want to stay and watch."

The bucket was detached from the end of the rope. The swearing, struggling drunk was promptly lowered into the well. His outcries became muffled, then ceased altogether.

"If he opens his mouth to yell now," said one of the crowd of wild celebrants, "he'll swaller the first water that's passed down acrost his tonsils since he was weaned off a milk bottle onto a whiskey jug. Don't drowned him, boys, he's my pardner and he owes me fifty dollars."

The windlass creaked as they hauled the dripping man up. He choked, sputtered, began a profane tirade.

"Down goes McGinty to the bottom of the sea," chanted the man at the windlass, and let go the handle. It spun like a pinwheel, paying-out rope. Dropping the man suddenly down like a plummet. And when they hauled the dripping man up again, he was sodden and limp as a rag. He was hauled over the edge of the box and the rope untied.

"Looks like his neck's broken," said a voice. Then the rasping voice of the drunken man's partner sounded a sinister rebuke to the big man who had handled the windlass.

"You dropped him a-purpose. You aimed to kill him. By God, you killed my pardner! Fill your hand!"

Almost at the same instant two guns spewed fire. The roar of the two shots blended. The big man at the windlass seemed to suddenly fold limply like an empty sack. The other man shot again into the falling body of the big man. Then he sank slowly on one knee and fell forward on his face, one outstretched hand almost touching the man he had killed.

The crowd, that had backed out of the line of fire, came cautiously forward. They examined the two still forms of the combatants.

"This 'un's deader'n a rock."

"He ain't got nothin' on the other feller. Hell, he's shot square in the briskit. He musta bin dead a'ready when he fired the second time."

The dripping inebriate was sitting up

now, unaware of what had happened, oblivious to what was going on around him. He rolled over on his hands and knees and commenced vomiting noisily.

Now for the first time Galt became aware of the fact that Nancy had shrunk against him and that he was holding her tightly in his arms as she hid her face against his chest. She was trembling a little and was clinging to him.

But before he could feel any emotion, embarrassment or otherwise, his eyes had focused on a man on horseback who had ridden into the yellow light that showed from the open doorway of the saloon. The man was Pecos Moss. And even as Galt recognized him, he whirled his horse and rode down the street out of sight.

For some moments Galt stood there, his arms around Nancy. And the faint, intoxicating smell of her hair was in his nostrils. It must have made him a little drunk for he lowered his hot face and buried it in her wavy hair. And when she lifted her face, he kissed her full on the mouth.

Nancy drew back, startled. Then, when he did not let her go, her arms tightened softly around his neck and she kissed him. Kissed him quietly, without passion, and her lips were smiling. He could see the starlight reflected in her eyes as she drew back her head a little. And her hands moved up to rumple his thick hair. Then she laughed softly at him, though there was color flooding her cheeks. "Do you kiss every girl you meet?" she mocked him teasingly, to cover her own confusion when she felt his arms trembling.

"Do you let every cowpuncher you're with kiss you?" he countered, his voice unsteady, dry in his throat.

Then they heard a commotion in the hall behind them. They had left the door partly open. And as they whirled, stepping away from one another, they saw men filling the lamplit hallway. Hushed voices and the clump of bootheels on the uncarpeted floor. They were carrying the two dead men into the Snake Room. And as one of them — Galt recognized him as Hipshot — unlocked the door of the Snake Room, there was a wild piercing shriek.

Hipshot whirled swiftly, his gun in his hand. The men carrying the two corpses had dropped their grisly burdens abruptly and clawed for their guns.

"Aunt Cloe!" gasped Nancy, and she ran for the hall door, Galt at her heels. And the next moment they were bending over the large, limp form that lay blocking the doorway from the hall into the upstairs parlor. Aunt Cloe had fainted dead away. . . .

"It ain't that I'm a-skeered of a dead stiff," explained Hipshot as he and Galt spread the new blankets and tarp Galt had bought, in an empty stall at the feed barn, "but somehow it don't seem exactly respectful to'rds the dead to be snorin' in the same room where they're laid out. Especially when we're plumb strangers to both of 'em."

Then he chuckled and slapped his lean leg. "Aunt Cloe won't never be the same no more. She'll be months a-gittin' her proper color back. Fer once she sighted me without accusin' me of bein' a pie thief. She'll be talkin' in a whisper fer days."

Then he took a drink from the bottle he had fetched along and stood with it in his hand, in the lantern light, looking taller and more loose-jointed than ever, standing "hipshot," his puckered eyes surveying Galt from head to foot.

"Fust time I got a good look at you, son. Ain't you the most duded up thing on two laigs! And you wear them store clothes like you was plumb broke and gentled into 'em. Now take most cowhands and put 'em into town duds and a white shirt and they'd look fer all the world like a mule a-lookin' over a whitewashed fence. But if you'd growed them duds they wouldn't fit you neater."

"They belonged to a tin-horn that got killed last week. He was about my size and the store man let me have 'em cheap. And a derringer pistol and gold nugget watch chain to go with it. Even his boots and hat was my fit. And the suit is tailor-made home-spun."

"Gamblers," said Hipshot, "is neat dressers. Only the ignorant goes in fer loud checkered pants and red ties. You're dressed as quiet as a preacher . . ." and he chuckled, his puckered eyes twinkling blue lights. He didn't dare tell the boy that Dodge was already calling him Gospel Galt.

"What did Nancy think of your fancy outfit?"

And as Galt's face reddened under its tan, the old range tramp went on ruthlessly:

"Near as I recollect, when Aunt Cloe liked to stampede me and the gents packin' the two stiffs with her panther squawl, you and Nancy come a-runnin' in off the roof. And Aunt Cloe was plumb alone in the front parlor when she got boogered . . ."

"I plumb forgot, Hipshot. Pecos Moss is

97

in town. I sighted him a-horseback, right after the shootin'.'"

Hipshot, with a quick movement, extinguished the lighted lantern. He spoke in a lowered voice in the darkness.

"You're plumb certain it was Pecos Moss, son?"

"Couldn't be mistaken. I got a good look at him. He rode off like he was in a rush. The light was dim down the street but I thought I saw him join three-four other horsebackers.

And they quit the main street and rode off between two buildings, and out of sight. Of course I'm wrong, but it looked like one of the riders was a woman, ridin' a sidesaddle. But that couldn't be."

"I ain't so sure but what you might be right. Though this is off her range, mostly. And I never heard her bein' mixed up with Pecos Moss. Still, there's the old sayin' about birds of the same kind of feathers, herdin' together. Ever hear tell of the Rose of Tascosa?"

Galt nodded there in the darkness. Hipshot talked in a low tone, and the young cowboy listened.

"I've never sighted her close. Mighty few men have, I reckon. And you kin hear almost any kind of story about her that you want to listen to. They class her with Belle

Starr and Calamity Jane and other women that ride with the outlaws. And they claim she has notches on her gun. On the other hand, there's others, poor folks among the Mexicans, mostly, that call her an angel. And the dance-hall girls of Dodge and Abilene call her their sister. One thing they all agree on. That she's as beautiful as a painting and calls no man her mate. Preacher Sam would have called her a Mary Magdalene. That was his name for women of her kind that didn't cook and wash and mend and raise a batch of kids and die, wore out and old at thirty. He was hard, thataway, on women, condeminin' 'em. Me and him never agreed on that. But that ain't the point right now. You've heard a lot of the wild tales about the Rose of Tascosa. And for its size, Tascosa is the wickedest little cow town on earth. And the headquarters of such men as Pecos Moss. And you think you sighted a woman with Pecos Moss and some other riders. You might be right. You might be more than right. . . ."

In the darkness there was a rasping note in the old range tramp's voice that Galt's quick ears caught. Hipshot was moved by some unusual emotion.

"We're wastin' time, Galt. If Pecos Moss is in Dodge, I'm findin' him. And I'll find out just what kind of a wildcat is this Rose of Tascosa that trails with low-down, bushwhackin' killers like Pecos Moss. Come on, son. And keep your hand near your gun. And on a hunt like this, there's a rule that's a safe 'un to foller. Shoot first and don't miss."

But if Pecos Moss or the notorious and mysterious Rose of Tascosa were in Dodge, they were well hidden. Galt and Hipshot searched until sunrise. And for some reason Hipshot kept the object of this seemingly aimless but actually tense search from Bat Masterson or any of Bat's deputies who kept an eye on things.

Hipshot's questions were carefully made. Bartenders, dance-hall girls, tin-horn gamblers, roustabout bar-room bums, the stable hands, cowboys. Nobody had seen Pecos Moss lately. The Rose of Tascosa? She never came to Dodge. What the hell? Tascosa was her town.

About sunrise Hipshot suggested they have breakfast. And get a little sleep if possible. . . . Before the two men who had been killed last night were planted in the Boot-Hill Cemetery. And Galt had winced a little.

Because, in their wandering from one saloon to another, and taking in the dance halls, in their search for Pecos Moss and the Rose of Tascosa, Galt had been hailed as "Gospel Galt" by a lot of men. And the dance-hall girls had eyed the tall, well-dressed youth with approving eyes. Perhaps it was in jest or there may have been something of sincerity about it all. At any rate, the man who had been dropped in the well last night, the man whose sorry plight had been the direct cause of the double killing, had sobered up somewhat. And with gold and pleading had sought the services of Gospel Galt.

"I'll give you the last dollar I got in the world, young feller, if you'll fetch along your Bible to the Boot-Hill and read somethin' out of it, there at the plantin'. It'd suit hell outa my dead pard. And it'll help me sleep better of a night, me bein' the cause of it. I got more'n a hundred dollars. And I'll throw in my pardner's horse and outfit to boot. Just read somethin' from your Bible, young feller, and you kin have the shirt off my back."

"Take him up on it," urged Hipshot. "A hundred dollars is money. He'd spend it on whiskey or the tin-horns 'ud take it off him, anyhow. What's that horse of your pardner's look like? Has he got ringbone or is he blind or mebby stole somewheres?"

"I don't want your money," said Galt, embarrassed by the crowd that had gathered, "or your pardner's horse. I'm no preacher."

"You pack a Bible," said the man stubbornly. "It's in your coat pocket. I kin see it."

Galt had put the small pocket Bible in his inside pocket for safe keeping. It made a bulge under his coat. More to escape the annoyance of the half tipsy man and the curious crowd, he agreed.

"If it will do any good," he had said, a little annoyed and self-conscious under the eyes of the crowd, "I'll do it."

He had to take a drink with the crowd. One of the dance-hall girls took him by the arm. A thin-faced girl with feverish eyes and splashes of color across her cheek-bones that was not artificial. She had a cough that told her tragic story.

"One of these nights," she said in a dry, colorless voice, "I'll have my last hemorrhage. Almost any night, now. I won't try to offer you money. But there's a God that'll pay you some day. And you'd be doing a kinder thing than you can possibly realize if you'd read a passage from your Bible, there at my grave, before they shovel the dirt in on top of my coffin. And if I can put in a good word for you after I get There . . . It won't be hell, because that's where I've lived now for five years. And they say that a sinner's prayer is as good as a saint's. I've got a nerve to ask you, but —"

"Oh course he'll do it," said Hipshot, who was standing at the bar next to Galt and had listened. "Won't you, son?"

"Yes."

The girl took Galt's hand in her two and pressed it hard. Then she dropped it and turned quickly away before the tears came to her fever-bright eyes and a fit of coughing gripped her. She left the place and they did not see her again. And only Hipshot had heard her desperate plea.

When Galt and Hipshot had left the place and were outside in the clean, fresh air, Galt said something which brought no reply from Hipshot.

"My mother was left here in Dodge. God knows what ever became of her. This is a hell of a place for a lone woman."

And because both of them knew the fear that lay behind Galt's words, that was why they could find nothing to say for a long time.

And now, at breakfast, in the hotel, Bat Masterson joined them. He had eaten, but took an empty chair at their table.

"One of the girls from the dance hall died just before daylight. Poor thing had lung trouble. She said before she died that you'd be at her funeral with your Bible, Galt. And we're burying her tonight after the moon comes up. She wanted it that way. She won't be buried at the Boot-Hill. But at the other graveyard. It's damned white of you, Galt. And don't ever be ashamed of Preacher Sam's Bible. Dodge could do with a few more Bibles and a few less guns. The moon should be up about ten. It'll be decent of you to show up."

"I'll be there."

Somehow Bat Masterson's words made Galt feel a lot better. Then the Marshal smiled faintly, his eyes on Hipshot.

"News trickled into Dodge sometime during the night, that Jeff Curtis has been killed. At least the note left shoved under my door said that somewhere between Las Vegas and the Canadian there was a new grave and Nancy Curtis would never see her father alive again. And that a rustler named Hipshot could take me to the grave if I used gun persuasion on him. What do you make of it?" He took a folded bit of paper from his vest pocket, unfolded it, and handed it to the old range tramp who passed it over to Galt.

"Read it, son. I ain't got my specs with me."
Galt read aloud:

Between Las Vegas and the Mill Iron camp on the Canadian is a grave. Shove a gun against a killer and horse thief named Hipshot and scare hell out of him and he'll pilot you there. And tell Jeff's daughter she need not wait no longer for him. Jeff made a bad mistake when he did not let the Vigilantes at Las Vegas hang that damn bushwhacker Hipshot. And young Magrath would not trail with Hipshot if he knew who killed Preacher Sam.

Galt quit reading. He looked at Bat Masterson. "The man that wrote this is a damned liar."

Bat Masterson nodded. "That's my opinion. But the man who left this note won't be satisfied with letting it go at that. Unless I'm badly wrong, Jeff Curtis has been killed. And the chances are his grave is marked. And within twenty-four hours we'll get news to verify just that. I've sent two men to the Mill Iron camp to investigate. They'll fetch back proof of Jeff's death. I'd bet on it.

"But that ain't all. The man who wrote

the note must have an ace in the hole. There'll be some sort of framed-up proof, Hipshot, that you killed Jeff Curtis. Chances are the proof will include Galt in the murder. And there'll be a lot of wild talk. The Mill Iron outfit will be in town. And some of those cowboys of his thought a lot of Jeff Curtis."

"And you're givin' us a chance to high-tail it, Bat?"

"All the proof they could show me wouldn't make me think you two killed Jeff Curtis. I know you better than most men do, Hipshot. And young Galt don't have the earmarks of a bushwhacker. But it might be just as well if you slipped out of town sometime tonight. Stayin' here would only mean trouble."

"Bat's right, son. We can't do no good here in Dodge. And when the sign is right, we'll slip out of town. Say about midnight. After the funeral of the dance-hall lady.

"Meanwhile, Galt, you find Nancy and stay close to her and Aunt Cloe and see that no damned sneak gits to 'em with any kind of news about Jeff. Keep hangin' around Nancy like a sandburr in a saddle blanket. Close-herd her and that nigger wench. I'll locate you when it's time to plant them two gents at the Boot-Hill. And you might practice some on a little sky-pilot talk. It might help your standin' as a' honest citizen if you preached a funeral sermon that these gents would like. And later on, if it come a tight, they'd be almighty hard to convince that a sky-pilot cowboy was mixed up in a bushwhackin' killin'."

"There's more truth than poetry in that," agreed Bat. "If you could use that Bible strong enough, it would be better than all the guns Colonel Colt ever made. Try it out. Practice on little Nancy and Aunt Cloe. There'll be a crowd at the Boot-Hill funeral. Doc Holliday and Mysterious Dave and the Hoo Doo Kid and Concho Jones and some more of the regulars will be there just for the hell of it. Convince them and you've got a backing. And to-night, when we bury the girl they called Virginia, there'll be a bigger crowd. There'll be a lot of folks there that nobody ever sees out in the light of day. The Virginia girl, because she's been sick a long time and the other girls have fussed over her like they would over a sick kitten, was mighty well liked. They're all going to her funeral. Somehow she'd even found a soft spot in that tough heart of Doc Holliday's. Give little Virginia the right kind of a send-off, and they'd tear any man apart that said a word against you. Hipshot's idea is all aces.

Think it over, Galt. And ride close herd on Nancy Curtis. See you later. Hipshot and I have work to do."

Upstairs, Aunt Cloe met him at the parlor door when he rapped a little timidly. She motioned him to silence and tiptoed out into the hallway, softly closing the door behind her. And she shoved a crumpled bit of paper into his hand. It was almost a duplicate of the one Bat Masterson had received and Galt had unthinkingly shoved into his own pocket.

"Somebody lef' it undah de do' las' night. Ah foun' it. Cain't read wif'out mah specs," she alibied as had Hipshot, not admitting she did not know how to read. "Is it bad news? Miss Nancy still sleepin' lak de lamb. Whut 'at note say, marse Galt, please?"

"It says," said Galt, thinking rapidly, "that Jeff Curtis has been killed. . . . Shhh. No noise. Whoever left this note was too much of a coward to deliver it himself. And chances are he's as big a liar as he is a sneak. And we're not gettin' Nancy all excited till we know the truth. You got to promise not to tell her a word about this note. And keep her from seeing anybody that might tell her. You don't want anybody hurting Nancy?"

"Ah'd bust 'em widah open dan 'at ol' rock Moses smote wif his stick an fotch fo'th watah by de barrel, dey hurt mah honey chile. Ain't lettin' nobody neah 'at baby. No sneakin' liah goin' say nothin' to mah chile — Lawdy, I plumb fo'got 'em daid co'pses in 'at room." And she opened the parlor door, breathing hard, and motioned feebly for Galt to follow. He was only too glad to do so. And hid his amusement as best he could. But Aunt Cloe was too scared to notice anything as she bolted the door. From the adjoining bedroom beyond came Nancy's voice.

"What's the racket, Auntie? Who banged the door? Ghosts?"

She opened the door and for a moment stood there in her nightgown, her wavy hair tumbled around her shoulders, below her waist. She gave a startled gasp as she closed the door.

And then, from the other side came her rippling laugh.

"So it was you busting in the door that I heard, was it, Galt? Trying to enter a lady's bedroom at daylight. Keep him covered with the shotgun, Aunt Cloe. If he tries to get in here while I'm dressing, defend my honor.

"So you slept out in the hall on the door-step?" she went on, talking through the closed door as she dressed. "And kept off the spooks. Which one of the corpses was it tried my door last night?" Nancy opened the door and poked her head through. Her hair was still a smoky black mass around her face.

"After we'd gotten Aunt Cloe pacified on Hipshot's bottle last night, and you'd gone, Galt, somebody tried our door. Aunt Cloe was asleep, and didn't hear. Because she was spooky, I'd left the light on, with the wick turned low. The house was quiet enough except for the usual town noises that don't keep us awake any more. The noises down in the street. Now and then a cowboy climbing the stairs and fumbling his way down the hall — But the man who tried the bedroom door wasn't drunk. He was sober enough not to make any noise. He walked tip-toe. One of his boots squeaked. I was wide-awake. Couldn't sleep. Too much excitement, no doubt." Her eyes lighted with mischief as she looked at Galt. He blushed hotly. Nancy smiled impishly and went on.

"I heard him stop at the parlor door first. I could hear fumbling noises. Stealthy, is a better word for the sounds he made. Then he came to the bedroom door that opens into the hall. He hadn't gotten in the parlor door, of course. I heard him stop by the door. I saw the doorknob turn cautiously.

But the door was bolted. I wonder if he'd tried if he knew I had a six-shooter covering the door. Anyhow, he went on his way. Stealthily as he'd come. One boot squeaking. Galt, do your boots squeak?" And with low-pitched laugh she shut the door.

"That was the gent that left the note," Galt whispered to Aunt Cloe. "Remember now. Keep the note a secret."

"Yes, *suh!*" and Aunt Cloe's eyes rolled. "Yuh-all don' reckon it coulda bin 'em co'pses a-playin' spook pranks?"

"It might have been," nodded Galt solemnly, "at that."

"Lawdy, Gawdy. Would yuh-all mind readin' a bit from yo' holy Bible? Ah'd feel a heap mo' unsqueamish."

VI

Galt spent most of the day upstairs in the "parlor" with Nancy and Aunt Cloe. And he always looked back upon it as one recalls a pleasant dream. Because he knew that Nancy's gay laughter would, in a few hours, be shadowed by grief. And he did all in his power to make these few hours before she heard of her father's death, as gay and pleasant as he possibly could. They talked and played cards with Aunt Cloe who enjoyed it all vastly.

Hipshot had told Nancy that Galt was to preach two funeral sermons. She insisted on his getting out the buckskin-covered Bible and preaching a special sermon to Aunt Cloe on spooks. The hours slipped past swiftly for Galt. He had never in his life met a girl like Nancy. He had, as a matter of fact, met very few girls in his life. And Nancy knew it and took advantage of his bashfulness. She teased Galt as she loved to tease Aunt Cloe.

When Hipshot came to get Galt, in late afternoon, about sundown, Nancy wanted to go along to the Boot-Hill. But old Hipshot would not let her. Mrs. Kelley, who ran the restaurant, was going to stay with Nancy and Aunt Cloe.

When the men came upstairs to take the dead men from the Snake Room, Aunt Cloe hid in a clothes closet. While Hipshot was in the hallway helping with the dead men, Galt and Nancy were left alone.

Without embarrassment, Nancy put her arms around Galt's neck and he kissed her, holding her close in his arms. And she was crying, her cheek buried against his shoulder.

"The day has been wonderful, Galt," she whispered. "Too happy to last. I'm afraid. Afraid that something terrible is going to happen to us. Galt, I'm scared. Hold me tighter."

"No matter what happens," he whispered as he held her tightly, "I want you to know I love you. I never told any girl that in my life, till now. There has never been any girl in my life. I love you, Nancy."

"I love you, Galt. You're coming with us

to Montana. Don't let anything happen to us, Galt. Don't ever leave me. You're so fine and clean and decent. Don't let anything change you. Take care of yourself. For me, Galt. I'm scared."

Hipshot rapped at the door. Galt kissed her. She clung to him a long moment, her lips hard pressed against his. Then she let him go. And when Galt joined Hipshot in the hallway, closing the door behind him, he heard a choked little sob, from the other side of the door. And somehow he knew that with the closing of her door he was shutting her away from him. And he shared her fear of impending disaster.

Downstairs their saddled horses were waiting. Hipshot spoke to Galt in a low tone.

"There's nothin' new in town, that I kin find out. But I'll bet a hat that the news has bin spreadin' that Jeff Curtis has bin killed and that me and you are mixed up in it. Men look at me sort of cornerwise when they think I ain't watchin'. Things is tightenin'. Walk careful."

They rode with the crowd to the Boot-Hill. The partner of one of the dead men was maudlin drunk. Nor was he alone in his tipsiness. More than one bottle was in the crowd that journeyed that evening to the

Boot-Hill. And as Hipshot had warned Galt, there were men in the crowd whose eyes were none too friendly as they watched Galt. And he was not a little relieved when Bat Masterson showed up with a couple of his men.

The sun was setting as Galt stood by the open grave and in a clear, modulated voice, read from his Bible. And with the open Book in his hand, said a few words.

No silly, maudlin sentiment. Only a brief little talk that lasted only a few minutes. He had prepared no sermon. Nor was this intended for any sermon. His were simple words, plainly said. And even the drunken partner of the dead man who was buried in the same grave as the man he had killed, seemed to sober up and listen.

When Galt had finished with his few words, he closed the buckskin-covered Bible and put it back in the inside pocket of his coat. Then he got on his horse and rode away with Hipshot.

"Preacher Sam hisself," said Hipshot, heading for the open country beyond town, "couldn't have done better." He took a bottle from the inside of his shirt and uncorked it.

Galt shook his head at the invitation. Hipshot grinned and drank. They rode on beyond the edge of town and along the bank of the Arkansas River. Here they halted and dismounted.

"It's goin' to be hell on her, son." Hipshot meant Nancy. Galt nodded. "Jeff was father and mother to her. You and her got acquainted right quick, didn't you, Galt? I ain't askin' to be nosey."

"We got to like each other right from the start, Hipshot." Galt's face reddened. But Hipshot wasn't going to josh him.

"I'm almighty glad of that, son. And I ain't blind. Ner deef. And just before I rapped on the parlor door to fetch you, I couldn't help but overhear a few words you and her was saying on yonder side of the door. Galt, you two was made for one another. I've knowed little Nancy since she was a yearlin'. Seen her grow up at the ranch on the San Saba. And I know there ain't a finer little girl on earth.

"Here's what you'll be up against before you're many hours old, the both of you. Lon Coulter's goin' to be in Dodge with the big news that Jeff Curtis has bin bushwhacked out of Las Vegas. And he's goin' to accuse me and you of the murder. And he's goin' to tell it almighty scarey to Nancy. He's her second cousin or some such distant kin. And he's goin' to make a strong play for her.

He's knowed her since she was a baby. And she's knowed him since she kin remember. And it's hard to tell just how much of what he'll tell her will git acrost. We don't know how much she'll believe. Lon is young and good-lookin' and a ladies man that practices at it. And he'll have a smooth brand of talk. He'll paint you and me blacker than a Dutch oven. And him bein' her nearest kin, he'll be her lawful guardeen.

"Me and Bat talked it all over. And Bat ain't no blinder than me, concernin' you and little Nancy. And what I'm telling you now is just what Bat and me agreed was the best thing for you to do. And it's this: Me and you slip out of town. We'll let Lon Coulter play his cards. Let him open the jackpot and bet 'em high. We're checkin' the bet to Lon, playin' our cards close to our belly, and keepin' our hole card buried deeper than hell. Let him think that he's got all the aces in the deck. And he'll overplay his hand or I'm no judge of men. He'll make a mistake somewheres and we'll jump him. We'll not only call his bet. We'll raise him higher than the moon. And when we push back our chairs, we'll have all the chips in the game. But we got to set back right now and let him run his whizzer. He's goin' to overplay his hand, sure as whiskey makes a man drunk.

117

"Ol' Hipshot has an ace up his sleeve, all the time. And what I think I know is so damned dangerous it's like a double handful of powder and a lighted cigaret in my mouth. It's too dangerous to let you in on. Because you might go off half cocked and spoil things. I'm not even tellin' Bat. I'm tellin' nobody. I got to play a lone hand."

"You think Lon Coulter ain't on the level?"

"I'd bet my last dollar he ain't. There was somethin' queer about that hoss stealin' Pecos Moss done when he taken them Mill Iron hosses. Lon Coulter wasn't expectin' to git back them ponies. And he had his own reasons for wantin' you and me hung before Jeff showed up. Lon Coulter and Pecos Moss was pardners in that deal. If Lon knowed the hosses belonged to Jeff, private, then Pecos likewise knowed.

"For some reason Jeff Curtis delayed his trail herd and went to Las Vegas, takin' with him a few men he could depend on in a tight. The only reason I kin think of that would make Jeff do a thing like that is that he hoped to find his brother Frank there. Jeff thought a heap of that wild son of a gun. For all Frank's wild ways, Jeff liked him. Though he let on to have cut him plumb loose and refused to let Frank even set foot on Mill Iron range. They didn't agree on things in general and quarreled bitter and hard. I was workin' for the Mill Iron when Jeff run Frank off with a gun. And I was with Jeff after Frank had gone and I know how hard he taken it. And I'm plumb positive that Jeff went to Las Vegas to locate Frank. But Frank wasn't there. And my bet is that Jeff was decoyed there by somebody who knowed Frank wasn't there. Frank wasn't in Las Vegas. Frank was in around Tascosa. Frank Curtis was wherever the Rose of Tascosa happened to be at that time . . . I didn't mean to tell you that much, but you might as well know. Frank Curtis, that was with the San Saba Pool, wasn't killed in the fight there on the Staked Plains. Either he got away or he was one of the rustlers. He's one of the outlaws that ride with the Rose of Tascosa. Some say he's married to her. *Quien sabe?* Who knows?"

"You think this Rose of Tascosa was in Dodge last night with Pecos Moss?" asked Galt.

"That's my guess. And if Pecos Moss is trailin' with her, then he knows a-plenty about Frank Curtis. And I'm guessin' fu'ther that it was Pecos Moss that got Jeff to ride to Las Vegas, usin' Frank as bait. I'm bettin' that Pecos Moss and the other rustlers was in Las Vegas, that night we turned Substantial Citizens, to kill Jeff. You and me kinda gummed the cards. They'd sighted us talkin' to Jeff in the restaurant. They tried to kill us before we got to talk much to Jeff. And the Vigilantes a-postin' that dodger likewise throwed sandburrs into Pecos Moss's batter. Pecos and two more curly wolves hit a high lope and headed for the Mill Iron camp on the Canadian. They talked it over with Lon Coulter without showin' up where the Mill Iron cowboys could see 'em meet and make medicine. Pecos either buffaloed Lon or worked some scheme to run off the Mill Iron remuda and set the outfit afoot. But they only got part of the cavvy because the nighthawk put up a fight and the shootin' fetched some of the cowboys to the rescue.

"Now I ain't accusin' Frank Curtis of bein' in on the hoss stealin'. Though Frank and Lon Coulter run together a heap. And they trailed plenty with Pecos Moss.

"But you kin lay all your coin that Frank never was in on ary deal to kill his brother Jeff. And if he was stealin' hosses, he figgered they belonged to the Mill Iron, not to Jeff, personal."

"You think Frank Curtis was with Pecos Moss and the woman called the Rose of

Tascosa when they were in town last night?"

"*Quien sabe?* It ain't likely. Because Frank just about worships little Nancy and he wouldn't have passed up the chance to pay her a visit. There's somethin' queer about it. Frank would have stopped to see Nancy. Bat has nothin' against Frank Curtis to keep Frank from comin' into Dodge, night or day. Coulter knows that Nancy is here. If he knows, then it's a cinch that Pecos Moss knows."

"And somebody else knows," said Galt, and told Hipshot about the note Aunt Cloe had found under the door. And how some man with a pair of squeaky boots had tried Nancy's door during the night.

"Here are the two notes. Printed, to disguise the handwriting. Both printed by the same pencil on the same kind of paper. Pages tore out of a tally book. I forgot to give back the one left under Bat Masterson's door. I'll give 'em both to him when we go back to town."

"We ain't going back to town, son. I got a loaded pack horse waitin' for us a few miles from here. That's what me and Bat decided after our medicine talk this afternoon."

"I promised that dance-hall girl that I'd be at her grave."

"Too big a risk, son. The whole town

121

knows you're to be there. And like as not Lon Coulter and a lot of Mill Iron men will be in town by then with the news about Jeff. Might be that Pecos Moss and some of his curly wolves will likewise be on hand. And before you could git your Bible open, they'll grab you and hang you to the nearest tree. "You know how sot Lon Coulter is on hangin' us."

"But this mornin' at breakfast you both said it would be a good idea to sort of preach a little sermon at the grave."

"That was this mornin' we said that, Galt. And things have begun gittin' tight since then. Only that they're waitin' for fu-ther orders, some of them jaspers at the Boot-Hill would have made a play then and there. But they're waitin' till moonrise to-night when you're supposed to be at the other graveyard to make a sky-pilot talk for the dance-hall gal Virginia. We'll out-fox 'em, son. Me'n you will be a long ways gone by moonrise."

"I gave that girl my promise, Hipshot. So did you. It don't seem decent to go back on our word. It meant a lot to her. I got to keep that promise, Hipshot."

Instead of heated opposition, Hipshot merely chuckled and took a drink.

"And I always claimed that Preacher Sam was the mule-headedest human that ever was set on earth. Damned if I ain't proud of you, son. You got principle. That's the word. Principle. You give your word. You keep it. You're keepin' your word to a dead lady. One of them that Preacher Sam called Mary Magdalene.

"Learn your piece by heart for the light won't be none too good to read the Bible by. And keep your gun hand on your hawg laig. I'll be somewheres in the shadder to back your play. This is goin' to be about the damnedest liveliest funeral Dodge ever attended at." He tipped up the bottle.

VII

Dodge City had two graveyards. Its famous Boot-Hill, where they buried men who died with their boots on. The other graveyard was for those who died less violent deaths. It was to the latter cemetery that they were carrying the earthly remains of the dance-hall girl called Virginia.

There was a round, white moon rising as the six men carried the coffin along the main street. They were gamblers and bartenders, the six picked pallbearers. Somberly dressed and decently sober, as befitted the solemn occasion. Behind them came a motley procession of men and women. The dance halls were closed. The saloons were all but deserted. Many were friends of the unfortunate dead girl. Still others were strangers who were drawn into the funeral procession by curiosity or other reasons.

For it had been common news in Dodge that Gospel Galt, a fighting cowboy sky-pilot, was to deliver a funeral sermon. And shortly after nightfall a sinister rumor had swept the town that if Gospel Galt showed up there were men waiting to grab him. Lon Coulter and a dozen or more Mill Iron cowboys had ridden to Dodge about dark, fetching with them the news that Jeff Curtis, trail drover and cowman, had been murdered. And that his murderers were one Hipshot, a range tramp and rustler, and his young partner, Galt Magrath.

Lon Coulter and his men had spread their talk. And Dodge City teemed with wild rumors. Bat Masterson and his deputies were non-committal, for the most part. Except that Bat had told the Mill Iron men and their friends that if there was any hanging done it would be done legal and not until after a jury trial had condemned the accused men after sufficient evidence was brought to court to prove guilt beyond all shadow of doubt.

"Jeff Curtis was a friend of mine," he told them flatly. "No man is more anxious than I am to punish his murderers. But it'll be done according to the law. Understand that. And I'm prepared to handle any hoodlums that try to take the law into their own hands.

Keep that in mind. Have warrants sworn out for Hipshot and Galt Magrath and I'll arrest 'em. Try any lynching tomfoolery and I'll deal you a bellyful of trouble. You can pass that on to Lon Coulter wherever he is."

Lon Coulter was up in the parlor of the hotel with Nancy and Aunt Cloe. He had gone there immediately after reaching town and after he and his men had learned that Galt and Hipshot had disappeared right after the double burial at the Boot-Hill. Making certain that Galt and Hipshot were nowhere to be found, he had gone to the hotel. And in the parlor upstairs had broken the evil tidings of her father's death to Nancy.

"Galt and Hipshot never killed my father," Nancy stubbornly insisted when her first terrible grief had abated enough for her to talk.

"I fetched proof along that they did, Nancy. I'm blaming myself plenty for not hangin' 'em when I had 'em prisoners for horse stealing. Hipshot has trailed with the Pecos Moss gang for years. And for the past two or three years this young Galt Magrath has been Hipshot's pardner. They were goin' to hang Hipshot at Las Vegas but he got away, with the help of this young Galt."

"I won't believe it until I hear it from Galt,

that he had anything to do with the killing of dad. And you can't make me believe that Hipshot did it, either."

"If they're innocent, why did they quit Dodge in such a hurry when they heard I was due in town?"

Then Aunt Cloe took a hand. She stopped her moaning and weeping and in no uncertain manner came to the defense of Galt. So militant was her attitude in defending Galt, who had read to her from his Bible and whose father had been Preacher Sam, that Lon had been forced to retreat. Aunt Cloe all but threw him out into the hall. And bolted the door after she had gotten rid of him.

Then she took Nancy in her huge arms and crooned brokenly to her. And the stricken girl found her only measure of comfort in the tears she shed with the old Negress who had been the only mother she could remember. The shock of Lon's death message had numbed the girl like a terrific blow. Dazed, she could not find even the solace of tears at first. And she had heard only part of what Lon was saying. And Aunt Cloe's moaning, as she sat in the old rocking-chair and covered her face with her apron and rocked back and forth, had added to the unreality of it all. Nancy could not think of her father as being dead. It must be some horrible mistake. It couldn't be the truth. Where was her father's dead body? Where was the proof of his death?

"You're lying! You're lying!" she had blazed out at Lon when she could find words.

Then he had accused Galt and Hipshot. And she had almost struck him across the mouth.

Lon Coulter, smarting under Nancy's words and humiliated by the treatment he had received from Aunt Cloe, stung by defeat when he had been so positive of success, cursed under his breath at the bolted door. And driven by an ugly, black temper, he had gone downstairs and out onto the street. He had been so sure of himself, that he had never for a moment taken any reckoning of defeat. He had pictured himself holding Nancy in his arms, comforting her. And her depending upon him, clinging to him, trusting him. He had pictured it countless times in his dreaming and planning. That she would not believe him, that she would shrink away from his touch, that she would let that fat nigger wench all but manhandle him, was preposterous, unheard of, impossible.

He wanted to be alone in his black hour of

bitterness. He didn't want to see or talk to any one. That damned black wench. She'd get her dose of bad medicine and get it before she could do any more harm. He wondered if the old fool suspected anything. She was wiser than most white folks suspected. Or what if Jeff had hinted anything to Nancy, back at the ranch on the San Saba. Though it was not like Jeff to talk things like that over with any one. Lon racked his brain for recollection of anything Jeff might have said or done in Nancy's presence to make her suspect that he, Jeff Curtis, had not trusted Lon very far. Hell, she couldn't suspect anything. She had let that young Galt and that oily-tongued old Hipshot talk their way into her good graces. That was the size of it. He'd heard how Galt had pulled his damned Bible business. And that damned nigger wench had fallen for the Bible like a kid for candy. Well, there'd be proof enough to hang old Hipshot and that young hero Galt. They'd hang quick enough. The Mill Iron men were steamed up plenty. They'd swallowed the yarn about the killing of Jeff Curtis. Pecos Moss had made a neat job of it all. Pecos had had tough luck with the horses. More tough luck at Las Vegas, thanks to Hipshot and Galt and the damned Vigilantes who had lucklessly picked that night, of all nights, to tack up a dodger and start a clean-up of their town. But he'd turned defeat into victory, after all. And killed Jeff and three of the Mill Iron men with Jeff. The other two men who had gone with Jeff from Las Vegas, on the trail to the Canadian, had been Pecos's men and had helped with the killing. And had fetched to the Mill Iron camp a fool-proof story of the attack from ambush by Hipshot and Galt. And because nobody on the outside knew the exact date of the murder, there was nobody to help Hipshot and Galt prove that they were Lon's prisoners the very night that Pecos and his two pardners, with one horse between them, on their way back to Las Vegas, had literally fallen into a pot of luck. They had sighted Jeff's camp-fire, had crawled up on it. Had spotted the two men who belonged to the gang and somehow managed to communicate with the two. And in the night Jeff Curtis and his three loyal men were killed without giving them any sort of fighting chance.

The story Pecos and Lon had fixed up had been ironclad. There could be no chance of a leak. And to eliminate even a remote chance of any slip-up, Lon aimed to have Hipshot and Galt strung up without delay.

Dodge City had been boiling over with

this news that Galt, now Gospel Galt to them, was going to preach a funeral sermon at the grave of a dead girl of the dance halls. And Lon hoped that young Galt would have the nerve to show up there at the graveyard. He and his pardner Hipshot. That would be the spot for his capture. If he showed fight, him and Hipshot, the crowd would kill them. And they'd be planted in the Boot-Hill as the murderers of Jeff Curtis. Lon choked back the muttered curses that were like lumps in his throat. He needed a drink. He needed more than one drink to wash the taste of bitter defeat from his mouth. But he had no desire to mingle with the saloon crowds. There was a bottle in his saddle pocket. His horse was tied behind the hotel. He avoided the crowd that was gathering for the funeral procession and slipped between the buildings and out back. And as he was standing in the shadow of his horse, the bottle in his hand, he gave a sudden start, almost dropping the bottle. He stared at a rider who came out of the shadows as he had appeared. The rider had gone behind the Beatty and Kelley Saloon, and then had ridden away at a slow lope. So that Lon had only a brief glimpse of him and his horse.

But that one, short glimpse was enough to

leave Lon Coulter shaken as if he had seen a ghost. And he needed a stiff drink to convince him that it was not a ghost riding that big, brown horse. Because the man on the horse was Frank Curtis. And only a week ago Pecos Moss had told Lon that Frank Curtis was dead. As dead as his brother Jeff, Pecos had sworn.

Lon uncorked the bottle with unsteady hands. And the raw whiskey had no taste as it went down his throat in big gulps. He must have swallowed nearly half a pint before he corked the bottle again. And he stood there, his hand on his gun, scowling at the crowd that was gathering in the street. Pecos had either lied or he had been badly mistaken about Frank. And if Frank Curtis was alive, then he was a menace far more dangerous than old Hipshot or Galt Magrath.

Lon had finished the bottle by the time he got on his horse and rode out to join the Mill Iron men who were riding past in the funeral procession.

From the balcony of the hotel, Nancy and Aunt Cloe watched the procession pass along, below in the street. Still numb and dazed by grief, yet unable to stay in her room, Nancy had gone out on the balcony-porch with Aunt Cloe. It was not idle curiosity that sent her out there. Nor could she have put her exact feelings into words, so chaotic and confused everything had become in her mind. But whatever her emotions were, her tear-reddened eyes searched the crowd that passed along below for a glimpse of Galt. And she had whispered to Aunt Cloe to watch for sight of him.

They spotted Bat Masterson and others they knew by sight, as they rode along in the moonlit street that was spotted with moving shadow. Nancy saw Lon Coulter riding with a group of Mill Iron cowpunchers. And there was something sinister and deadly about the way they sat their horses, their hands near their guns.

Then the last of the funeral procession had passed. And they had seen no sign of Galt nor Hipshot.

Nancy went back inside, the colored mammy close behind her. Back in the bedroom the girl ripped off her dress and pulled on shabby, service-scarred riding clothes. A flannel shirt and men's cowboy pants. Boots and a man's hat. Tucking her hair up under the high crown. While Aunt Cloe watched in a numb sort of stupefaction.

"Honey chile, wa' —"

"You have to stay here, Aunt Cloe. I'm going to the cemetery. In the night nobody will recognize me for a girl. Can't you see, I *just have* to go!"

And before Aunt Cloe could protest, Nancy was gone. Downstairs and out onto the street. She ran to the barn. It was deserted. She found her horse and saddled swiftly. Leaving the feed barn, she swung off the main street at a run and before the long procession had reached the graveyard she had caught up with it. She rode astride like a man, and with her hat pulled low across her eyes, so that the upper part of her face was in the shadow, and a big silk neckscarf partly concealing the lower part of her face, nobody, not searching closely, would have recognized her as a girl, there in the uncertain light. She slipped in among the other riders unobtrusively. Nobody paid any attention to her. She looked like any other cowboy, in her rough clothes. Even to the six-shooter she wore in a holster fastened to a filled cartridge belt.

She sat her horse, watching for sight of Galt. Other riders were grouped around her. Beyond was the open grave. The six pallbearers had set down the coffin which was a pine box painted white. They stood there, a little awkwardly, looking around and straightening their backs. All were armed with six-shooters.

The girls from the dance halls stood in a group on the other side of the open grave. They had bunches of homemade artificial flowers to toss in on top of the coffin.

There was no sign of Galt or Hipshot. Bat Masterson sat his horse, looking over the crowd from under his slanted hatbrim. He stared hard at Lon Coulter and the Mill Iron cowboys who stayed bunched. Nancy caught a glimpse of Lon's face. A shade white from too much whiskey, drawn in a faint, mirthless grin. And his voice was harsh and a little loud.

"Looks like the sky-pilot thinks more of his neck than he does his preachin'. It'll take more than a Bible to git him clear of murder." Lon spoke to the Mill Iron cowboys but his voice carried across the crowd in the hush that had fallen.

The barber called Sport McAllister was there with a following of cronies. Beer slingers, tin-horns, "professors" from honkeytonks, parasites. Bandaged, half drunk, armed, he had made threats against Galt and was waiting his chance. It was this crowd, and the Mill Iron cowhands, that Bat Masterson watched closest.

Doc Holliday, Mysterious Dave, Dog Kelly, the Hoo Doo Kid and other real gamblers formed a group apart. And Doc was

135

still betting that Galt would show up.

"Even money that Gospel Galt shows up," he said to Lon Coulter. "I'll call any amount. I heard your war cry, mister. Now back it with money or shut up." His tone was flat, deadly. It was said of Doc Holliday that he was the most dangerous man in Dodge.

"My share of the trail herd and remuda in the Lazy J road iron," said Lon. He hadn't meant to say it. That had been whiskey talk. And the Mill Iron men stared hard at him. For, so far as they knew, the herd and remuda belonged to the Mill Iron. Only a few of them, members of the Pecos Moss gang, knew anything else.

"Call that," snapped the gambler. "Who else has sportin' blood in their veins?"

None of the Mill Iron men spoke. The battered barber bet a hundred. One or two others made small bets. Bat Masterson smiled grimly.

Nancy had heard Lon's bet. And wondered what he meant by his share of the cattle and horses that had belonged to Jeff Curtis. Lon had no share in the herd or the remuda. . . .

Then Galt Magrath rode up. Nobody had seemed to notice his coming. He just seemed to appear. A moment before there had been no sign of him. Now he was here.

Alongside Bat Masterson. Sitting his horse straight-backed. Hands on the pommel of his saddle.

Nor did Bat Masterson seem greatly surprised. He grinned faintly and nodded. Galt dismounted, handing his bridle reins to Bat. And with his Bible in his left hand, walked to the head of the open grave.

A murmur ran like a rippling wave across the tense crowd. Galt's appearance had been so abrupt it caught his enemies off-guard. And not even the drunken barber had the temerity to voice threats or make a move. Lon Coulter's face had gone a yellow, chalky color.

Doc Holliday smiled thinly. His two hands had dropped to his guns. And he spoke to Lon Coulter in a low monotone.

"Interrupt Gospel Galt and I'll kill you, mister. I'm collectin' all bets to-morrow."

Nancy swayed dizzily in her saddle and had to grip the saddle horn with both hands. She was staring at Galt who had dropped his hat on the ground and stood there, tall and straight, his head erect, the open Bible in his two hands.

"God in Heaven!" gasped a woman's voice from somewhere near at hand. And the voice was so tense, so filled with emotion, that Nancy's gaze was torn from Galt.

She saw a woman on a beautiful black horse. The woman rode a side-saddle and was dressed in soft, brown buckskin. A man's black hat was on her head, shading the upper part of her face. But in spite of the dim light, Nancy knew that the woman was beautiful. The moonlight glinted on a mass of thick hair the color of burnished copper. One gloved hand was gripping the long mane of the black horse. And she was staring at Galt, tense, breathless.

There were men around her. Bearded, most of them, and heavily armed. And it was part of this group of men who were nearest Nancy.

"The Rose of Tascosa," said one of them, "looks like she sighted a ghost."

"Not a bad guess at that," muttered a voice that Nancy recognized with a start. And turned her head so that the light of the moon was full in her white face. And reached out one hand to old Hipshot.

Hipshot's seamed face was so changed that she hardly recognized him. He looked at her without seeming, for a moment, to know her. And his puckered blue eyes went back to stare at the Rose of Tascosa. His mouth was twitching oddly under his drooping mustache. And there was a six-shooter in his hand.

"What the hell you doin' here?" he hissed at Nancy. "As if we ain't got enough on our hands. Git over to Bat Masterson. *Pronto.*"

Then Hipshot, his gun still gripped in his hand, rode through the crowd and shoved his horse alongside that of the outlaw queen called the Rose of Tascosa. While Nancy, as if gripped by a hypnotic spell, watched.

She saw the woman give a start. Then Hipshot shoved his gun back in its holster and gripped her arm as she swayed a little. Nancy saw her smile faintly and let go the mane of her horse to grip Hipshot's hand.

Then Galt was talking. And Nancy's glance sped back to him. And Hipshot's orders to go to Bat Masterson went unheeded as she stared, listening to Galt's voice.

Gospel Galt talked. His voice was clear, steady, vibrant. He talked as if he believed every word he said. And there was no fire and brimstone, no hellfire and damnation in his simple phrasing. He spoke of the girl who had died as if she had departed on a pleasant journey to a place where her hardships would be forever forgotten. Where there was only rest for her weary heart, and comfort and understanding. No mention of Mary Magdalene. No word of her sins, her shortcomings. She had been their friend here on earth, no better, no worse than those here at her last resting place. God had created her. God understood and forgave his children their trespasses. God punished evil, to be sure. But He rewarded good, also. And He was just and kind and tolerant.

It was not a sermon that Galt preached. He told them that he was no preacher of God's teachings. He had a Book that had belonged to his father. The dead girl had asked him to read from it. He was no sky-pilot. He had kept a promise to a girl called Virginia, a stranger.

Galt closed his Bible and picked up his hat. He walked over to his horse and took the bridle reins from Bat Masterson.

"I understand I'm bein' accused of the murder of Jeff Curtis," he said in a quiet tone that carried to the ears of every listener. "I'm placin' myself under arrest to face the charges against me." He swung into the saddle.

"Do I surrender my guns?"

"Keep your guns, son," said Bat Masterson.

The Marshal of Dodge motioned to Lon Coulter.

"I understand you're the man that accuses Galt Magrath of murder? Is that right?"

"Yes. I'll fetch proof enough to hang him

and his pardner Hipshot. They killed Jeff Curtis!"

This was not at all as Lon Coulter had planned things. He felt as if he were playing a losing hand. He had not reckoned on Galt's surrender. He had not wanted it that way. A quick lynching had been his plan. But there was nothing for it but to make the best of things.

Then Nancy spurred her horse through the crowd. Her face was pale, her eyes blazing. Galt stared at her blankly. Her shouted words struck him like a blow across the face.

"You're a rustler and a liar, Galt Magrath. Lon was right. I hope they —"

The words died unspoken in her throat. She reeled in her saddle. Only that Bat Masterson grabbed her she would have fallen to the ground. For Nancy Curtis had fainted dead away.

Too dazed for the moment to understand, Galt sat his horse, staring blankly. And then he realized his danger. Nancy's accusation had suddenly altered everything. Lon Coulter, quick to follow up the advantage fate had thrown in his favor, yelled something to the Mill Iron cowboys. But before they could go into action, Galt whirled his horse, digging the spurs in. And the next instant he was

141

riding at a run, Hipshot and some other men with him. Hipshot was cussing as he rode alongside Galt. Behind them was confusion. Shouts. Some wild shooting.

"Keep a-spurrin'," said Hipshot, grinning and scowling at the same time. Galt's right hand held a six-shooter now instead of a Bible.

As three or four men crowded close, he swung sideways in his saddle, to fight. Hipshot, riding alongside, barked at him.

"Hold your fire, son! They're all right!"

"Who are they, then?"

"Friends of mine. They belong to the gang that takes orders from the Rose of Tascosa."

As they rode at a run through the night the men who had come with Galt and Hipshot dropped behind, one or two at a time. Until the two were riding alone. Hipshot acted a little drunk and not quite in his right mind, it seemed to Galt.

The old range tramp kept muttering and cussing to himself, alternately chuckling and scowling.

"What brand of forty rod have you been samplin'?" asked Galt. "And will you tell a man how the Rose of Tascosa's men happened to be there at the funeral?"

"And right back at you, son. What in hell

was the idee in givin' yourself up to the law thataway when there wasn't even a warrant out for yuh? That wasn't in the deal, as we talked it over with Bat. And what in hell got into Nancy that she turned on you like a rattler?"

"Nancy," said Galt bitterly, "judgin' from the way she acted, believed the story her handsome cousin Lon told her. That was plain enough even for a thick-skulled fool like me to savvy. She throwed in with Lon Coulter plenty strong."

"And after that Bible talk that even had me almost swearin' off good likker and throwin' my guns away. Who fetched her there, anyhow?"

"She come with Lon, of course. You don't think I took her? If she hadn't horned in, my plan might have worked. I figured that if I turned myself over to Bat Masterson, it would force Lon's hand in a fair court of law. He can't prove that we killed Jeff Curtis. Bat wouldn't stand for a lynching. We'd stand a fair trail and come clear."

"Next thing," growled Hipshot, "you'll tell a man you believe in Santa Claus and the stork. Lon's got framed evidence that'll hang us. He ain't makin' that talk without some sort of backin'. Hell. . . . But son, I'm proud of you. I never heard a finer talk. You have Preacher Sam skinned a mile."

"Yeah. Nancy Curtis shore ate it up, didn't she?" Galt's short laugh was more like a bark.

"Mebbyso it didn't make so much of a hit with her. But it was plenty good enough for the Rose of Tascosa. . . . And they say that she don't believe in God ner preachers."

"Who is this Rose of Tascosa?" asked Galt, interested in spite of the hurt that galled him like a raw wound. "What was she doin' there? Did you meet up with her?"

"I don't know how come she happened to be there unless she come to hear you preach. Mebbyso she knowed the dead gal. I was talkin' to her, when you commenced preachin'. She knowed that Lon Coulter was accusin' us of Jeff's murder. And when she seen you was in a tight, she told her curly wolves to handle Lon and his cowboys and cover our gitaway. Which they shore done. And I don't think there was ary killin', either. Them men that take her orders are seasoned. They got orders to kill only when they're crowded. And don't ask me no questions because I wouldn't know the right answers. We'll meet her at Tascosa to-morrow night."

"At Tascosa?"

"Near there. At her place on the Canadian, a few miles down the Canadian River

144

from town. We're to meet her there and make medicine."

"Listen, Hipshot, I'm not throwin' in with her and her rustlers."

"Then dammit, go back to Las Vegas and join them Substantial Citizens," rasped the old range tramp hotly.

"Because Nancy Curtis called me a rustler is no sign I'm goin' to be one," insisted Galt stubbornly.

Hipshot cussed under his breath and fished out a bottle. He took a big drink and they rode on in a silence that was charged with wordless anger.

It was the first time they had ever really quarreled seriously. And it was what they left unsaid, rather than the brief exchange of hot words, that now was causing the trouble.

Hipshot had never before hinted that Galt turn outlaw. And the young cowpuncher somehow blamed the woman called the Rose of Tascosa for the old range tramp's attitude. Never before had Hipshot acted as he was acting now. As if he was loco drunk.

Galt finally broke the strained silence. "You're aimin' to throw in with that she-outlaw and her renegades?"

"I give her my promise that we'd meet her to-morrow night at her ranch below

Tascosa," growled Hipshot sullenly.

"After this, when you make promises, don't include anybody but yourself. Join her. Trail with your friends, the rustlers. I got other ideas."

Galt reined his horse around and rode off at a lope, headed in a direction at right angles to the south-by-west course Hipshot had taken from Dodge. It was a hotheaded, childish thing to do. But he was not quite in his right senses. Nancy's accusation, coming as it did, had jarred him off balance. He wanted to be alone. He resented even Hipshot's presence.

Ordinarily old Hipshot would have grinned and followed. For that matter, had old Hipshot been thinking with his customary clarity, there would have been no quarrel.

But the abrupt meeting with the woman called the Rose of Tascosa had been a terrific shock and he was still in a state of bewilderment. Too, he had put away a lot more whiskey on an empty stomach than he had realized. He was more than a little drunk. Drunk on whiskey and emotion.

Because the Rose of Tascosa was the girl he had known as Mary Galt, who had married Preacher Sam. The Rose of Tascosa was Galt Magrath's mother!

VIII

The resentful, sullen anger that seethed within Galt, drove him on through the night, his horse settling to a long, tireless trot that ate up the miles and put distance between him and old Hipshot. And by the time that anger had cooled and he was feeling heartily ashamed of himself, it was too late to turn back. He was on a strange range. More or less lost, though he had his sense of direction. That, in spite of the fact that the sky had slowly blackened and not even a single star was visible in the sky that was pregnant with rain. But he reckoned that he must be nearing water. Probably Bluff Creek, that emptied into the Cimarron.

By the light of sheet lightning he read the hands of the stem-winder watch Hipshot had won in a poker game and given him for a present. It was two o'clock in the morning.

He reckoned he had covered at least twenty-five or thirty miles since leaving Hipshot, for he had been riding hard. Only the last few miles he had slowed down. The watch reminded him of old Hipshot and he felt like a coward and a quitter and many other hard names that he called himself. He reckoned he'd camp when he reached some sort of natural shelter. It was beginning to rain. Big drops of it wet his hands and face. With a mirthless grin he became aware of the fact that he was still wearing his new town clothes. His old clothes were tied behind his saddle cantle. The clothes made him remember. Nancy. She had admired the tailored suit. He had half a mind to throw 'em away. Instead, he dismounted and slipped off the coat and vest and pants and put on his old range clothes and a new rough flannel shirt. And, rolling his town clothes in a neat, tight bundle, wrapped them in a cavalry poncho he had bought in Dodge, and tied the bundle on his saddle. He'd keep his new clothes dry at the cost of taking a cold drenching when the storm broke. With a boyish touch of love-sick bitterness he told himself he'd cut a few fancy pigeon wings with the dance-hall girls at Tascosa. For he had decided to head for that wicked little cow town when he got his bearings, come daylight. He'd find Hipshot at Tascosa. And hell, if the Rose of Tascosa had liked his preaching as much as Hipshot claimed, he'd shine up to her. He'd show Nancy Curtis that she wasn't the only girl in the world.

For, after all, despite the fact that he was a grown man in stature, and was matured in most ways, he was still a boy in his way with a girl. And he was so much in love with Nancy that he was almost physically sick from her treatment of him. Galt Magrath, just now, was taking himself almighty seriously.

Then the storm broke with a ferocity of hail and wind that drove him and his horse before it. Hailstones as big as hen eggs, hard as ice, pounded his back and head and shoulders, and made his horse jump and hump up and snort. Then the horse found a cutbank that afforded a little shelter. Galt swung to the ground and crouched in the lee of the clay bank, hanging to the hackamore rope. And let the storm do its worst.

He did not know how long the hail lasted. It seemed a long time. And the wind was a gale. Then the rain came in sheets and the lightning split the black sky apart. Thunder deafened Galt's ears. In no time he was standing almost waist deep in the swift torrent that came down the shallow coulée.

And he wondered what was happening to the Mill Iron herd that he heard was camped on the Cimarron, about fifty miles south of Dodge City. Because a storm like this is apt to cause a stampede. And Hipshot, who had ways of finding out many things, had learned back in Dodge that Lon Coulter had fetched all the cowhands excepting about half a dozen, that included the night-hawk and day wrangler, to town with him to capture Hipshot and Galt. Half a dozen men can't hold a big trail herd and a remuda of almost two hundred head of horses, when a bad storm like this breaks loose.

"There'll be cattle and horses scattered from hell to Texas," Galt told himself. It gave him something besides his own personal troubles to occupy his mind. And because his mind was that of a cowhand, he became engrossed with this fresh line of thought. The storm was coming from the north. The cattle and horses would naturally be wanting to drift back towards their home range. And once the stampede had scattered them, this storm would drift them in the direction they wanted to go. Back to Texas.

"Scattered like a sheepherder's thoughts," grinned Galt. "It'll take Lon Coulter and his men a week of Sundays to gather 'em.

Gather what the rustlers don't find and run off."

Galt got a lot of pleasure in this gloating over his enemy's bad luck. Until he suddenly remembered that the cattle and horses now belonged to little Nancy Curtis. And his satisfaction turned to something quite different.

No matter how shabbily she had treated him, Nancy didn't deserve this streak of bad luck. Her father's death. Lon's lies poisoning her mind. And now the trail herd scattered to hell and gone. And a remuda of picked top horses at the mercy of rustlers. And she'd be stranded there in Dodge City with only that lying, thieving son of a snake Lon Coulter to tie onto. That was hell for a girl. She was getting as tough a break as the wife Preacher Sam had left stranded there at Dodge. Poor youngster. It wasn't right. No wonder a lot of folks didn't believe in God.

"I'll cut Hipshot's sign at Tascosa," he told himself as he quit the shelter of the cutbank, "and he'll figure out something." Old Hipshot always could scheme out of a tight. He'd show Nancy that he and Hipshot were men. Then he'd tell her good-bye for keeps and ride off. . . . Galt's youth was again asserting itself in his reckoning.

He swung into the saddle and drifted with

151

the storm. And after a long time, the rain slackened to a drizzle. He was drenched, chilled to the marrow of his bones. His boots were filled with water, and his feet were like clubs of ice. Cold numbed his cramped hands. Shivering, sodden, he rode humped in the saddle like a hunchback.

Then, when the country became broken and he knew that he was following a creek, he spotted a light in the distance, through the drizzle and darkness that precedes the dawn.

He started to quicken the pace, then caution pulled him to a halt. He swung around in the saddle and untied the saddle strings that fastened his poncho and dry clothes to the saddle. And spent some minutes drying his six-shooter on the dry clothes. And then he reloaded his six-shooter with cartridges that had been in the poncho-sheltered cover. He knew that moisture shouldn't harm the brass shelled cartridges, but he was taking no chances. A light meant men and men, he had learned long ago, meant danger. He cut off a big square of the poncho and wrapped it around his gun, carrying it in his hand. One quick flip and the dry gun would be free of its rain-proof covering and ready for use.

Then he rode on towards the light.

The light came from an old sod cabin. It had no door, no covering for the single small window. The light came from a buffalo-chip fire in the adobe fireplace.

Galt made out the shadowy blots of three saddled horses standing inside an adobe corral. There were a few trees around. He left his horse and, removing his chaps and spurs to make walking easier and more quiet, he tied them to his saddle. Then he slipped through the darkness towards the cabin. And through the window he made out three men squatting on the dirt floor in front of the fire. They had a jug of whiskey from which they took turns drinking. They talked in tones made loud by the corn whiskey, and Galt knew that the storm had driven them here to the deserted sod cabin for shelter. He recognized two of them as men Hipshot had pointed out to him somewhere in their travels as rustlers. The other was a Mill Iron cowhand who had backed Lon's urgent desire to hang Galt and Hipshot when they had been his prisoners. The Mill Iron man was talking.

"Lon is goin' to take the damnedest losin' of his life before Pecos is done with him. And Pecos is plumb right, to my notion. It ain't buyin' him nothin' to lollygag around the girl. Hell, what he's after is the cattle and

153

horses that belong to Jeff Curtis. Lon aims to marry them cattle and horses when he marries Jeff's daughter. Pecos claims it's a damn sight easier to run the cattle and horses off, like the San Saba Pool herd was run off. Sell 'em and split the money, payin' us boys off at fightin' wages. And that's where Pecos Moss shows sense. Plenty much sense.

"So he ribs Lon into takin' what Mill Iron men that's loyal to Jeff and Jeff's daughter, and headin' for Dodge. While them that he leaves behind on the Cimarron with the herd is like us boys, all for Pecos Moss. So while Lon Coulter is in Dodge killin' off Hipshot and that Galt feller, Pecos and his boys drifts the cattle *and* the best damn remuda that ever come out of Texas, off the bedground. And hazes 'em back to Tascosa, on the Canadian. Where he delivers 'em at a hell of a good price to the lady they call the Rose of Tascosa. Her and Pecos is thicker than two blanket-Injuns, since Frank Curtis got killed and left her without a handsome cowboy pardner. And if that damned fool Lon Coulter gits snuffy and cuts their sign, Pecos will fill his belly full of lead. Pecos Moss has done all the hard, dangerous and dirty work. And he ain't the loco fool to cut Lon in on the hard-earned proceeds. Nope.

Lon Coulter has done lost hisself a trail herd. And without her cattle, Jeff Curtis's gal ain't no value to purty Lon who takes his pick and choice of petticoated fillies. The joke's on Lon. Pecos Moss just nacherally sent that purty cowboy on a snipe hunt. Lon's a-holdin' the sack right now in Dodge. Let's drink."

"To the Rose of Tascosa," toasted the cowboy who had the jug. "Queen of the outlaws and the rustler's guardeen angel."

"She picks her men from the top-hands. She kin pick on me any time," added the other cowhand. "I seen her once. Purtiest thing I ever laid eyes on. Sorrel-colored hair longer than a horse's tail. And she don't believe in God ner the sky-pilots that peddle His gospels."

"And for a damn good reason," leered the Mill Iron man, taking the jug and wiping the palm of his hand across its wet opening.

"Meanin' how, pardner?"

"Meanin' that she got kind of sick and foundered on too much preachin' in her younger days. Before she was known as the Rose of Tascosa. Before she trailed with Frank Curtis and now with Pecos Moss. Gawd knows how many other men she's strung along with before now. She don't believe in God ner his rules and regulations.

But she did once upon a time. When she was married to a circuit-ridin' sky-pilot called Preacher Sam Magrath!"

"What?" barked one of the men.

"If Frank Curtis wasn't dead, he could tell you more than that. And he might tell you the reason that Preacher Sam was killed was on her account. Because that mealy-mouthed psalm singer had kicked her out and left her stranded in Dodge to be looked after by the ladies and gents of that cow town which Preacher Sam called the worst hell hole on the face of the earth since the Bible days of a couple of wild towns called Sodom and Gomorrah. I got my information straight. From somethin' I overheard Frank Curtis and the Rose of Tascosa sayin' once. And I ain't ashamed to say that while Frank was alive, I didn't peddle the secret. He'd have cut my heart out. Gents, here's drinkin' to the queen of the rustlers. The red-headed Rose of Tascosa!"

But he did not drink. The jug dropped from his hand and lay on its round belly, the whiskey gurgling out of its neck. He was staring wide-eyed at the sodden figure that filled the doorway, standing just inside. The other two, quick to scent danger, turned. But none of them drew their guns.

Because the gun in Galt's hand seemed to cover each of them.

No man of them spoke. There could be no words. Only this tense silence. Then guns would blaze and there would be blood and powdersmoke and death.

Galt crouched a little, his gun in his hand. His face was gray, distorted as if from some tearing, burning torture. His bloodshot eyes stared at the three men with a tensity that seemed to have a hypnotic spell, for they sat as if frozen there. Their eyes looked at death. His right hand gripping his gun, he pointed stiffly with his left at the Mill Iron man who had divulged the identity of the notorious Rose of Tascosa.

"You!" Galt croaked. "Stand on your legs. Fill your hand. I can't kill you sittin' down."

But the man didn't move. "Christ! It'll be murder!" he whispered, and his rasping words filled the sod cabin.

"Stand on your legs!"

Then, outside in the black drizzle, a gun cracked. Galt's knees buckled and he sprawled forward on his face. He lay there, a widening spot of blood showing on his forehead, staining the gray pallor of his skin, just under the line of his thick hair under his hatbrim.

Then the head and shoulders of Pecos

Moss showed in the square hole meant for a window. His bleak eyes were hard. The faint grin on his rain-wet face mocking the three staring, dazed men.

"Come on, you three drunken, clumsy fools. Get out of there. Get your horses."

They needed no urging, these three men who had looked into the eyes of death. The Mill Iron man stepped over the motionless form of Galt with a quickness that brought a short, rasping laugh from Pecos Moss.

"Scared of Galt Magrath even after he's dead, eh, Windy?" sneered Pecos Moss. "Damned lucky for you that I sighted the light and rode here. I don't know just how you three *muy valiente hombres* got into the tight but you looked for all the world like three rabbits. And that son of a sky-pilot was a coiled rattler. How'd he git here? Lon was supposed to gather in him and Hipshot and wipe 'em out. What was he doin' here? Where's his pardner Hipshot?"

But the Mill Iron man he had called Windy had no explanation. He shook his head stupidly. He hadn't gotten over his close call with death. And the whiskey he had drunk was making him a little sick from that reaction of stark fear. He wanted to vomit and did, as they got their horses and rode away into the black drizzle.

Pecos Moss was in an ugly, surly mood. And not a little worried. Neither he nor the three men who had taken shelter at the sod house, knew what had happened at Dodge. They had been headed for the Mill Iron camp on the Cimarron to meet there and take the trail herd and remuda. The sudden storm had been an uncounted factor. Pecos reckoned that the herd was probably stampeded and scattered to hell and gone by now.

He had sighted the light at the sod cabin and had slipped up on it, much after the same fashion Galt had. To hear Galt's rasping command. A glance through the window had shown him the situation. He had fired without hesitation. And had seen Galt go down like a shot beef. And though that shooting had given him some satisfaction, still Hipshot was unaccounted for. And Hipshot had the annoying habit of being somewhere in the vicinity where you found Galt. Pecos had a wholesome respect for the old range tramp's prowess as a gun fighter. Better to quit the vicinity of the sod cabin.

They left without trying to locate Galt's horse or to make a search for Hipshot. Pecos was anxious to reach the Cimarron and see what had happened to the trail herd and remuda. He cursed the storm as he rode away from the sod cabin. There was no doubt whatever in his mind that Galt was dead. Pecos prided himself on his marksmanship. He belonged to that glory hunting, swaggering breed that brags of their killings. So as he rode he took his knife and cut a notch in the cedar handle of his six-shooter. That made him feel a little better.

IX

But Galt Magrath was not dead. The bullet had grazed his skull, cutting a furrow an inch or two long in his scalp. As his eyes blinked open he was almost blinded by red, stabbing pains in his head. He sat up dizzily, groping for his gun.

A drawling voice came out of the shadows somewhere in the cabin. The fire had died down, leaving only a dull red glow that did not reach the man who stood near the doorway, a gun in his hand. Though Galt was within its dim red light.

"If you're huntin' your gun," said the voice that Galt could not recognize as ever having heard before in his life, "don't bother. I got it. And just set there quiet, as long as you ain't dead. And don't lie when you answer my questions. First, who are you?"

"That's what I'd like to ask you," said Galt.

"I'm askin' the questions. And I don't want a lie. Who are you? I'd advise you to talk up."

There was something deadly and compelling about that unhurried Texas drawl. Galt's brain began to function. If the man was asking his identity, then he didn't belong with the three men who had been here in the sod cabin. He wondered what had happened to them. And he wondered who had hit him over the head or shot him. One moment he had been standing there in the cabin, ready to kill that big Mill Iron skunk he'd known as Windy. Then blackness and oblivion. Now this man he could not make out for the darkness was asking him his name. And there wasn't time to think up a false one.

"My name is Galt Magrath."

"The hell you say! I told you not to lie, mister. Galt Magrath is in Dodge. Him and his pardner Hipshot. Gospel Galt, they're callin' him. He's in the Dodge jail or else he's swingin' at the end of a rope. I'll give you one more chance to tell the truth. Lie and I'll finish the job somebody left half done."

"I have no way of provin' who I am —

Hold on a minute. If I show you the Bible that belonged to my father, you'd take my word for me bein' Gospel Galt. Unless the three snakes that left me for dead here stole it. . . . They didn't. Here. Here's the Bible. And if you're one of Pecos Moss's gang, you'll kill me for provin' who I am." He got to his feet groggily, the Bible in his hand.

"Stand where you are," said the man. "I'll take your word for bein' Galt Magrath. Though it sounds almighty queer. I never met Galt Magrath. I knowed Preacher Sam. And I know Hipshot. And I know. . . ."

"The Rose of Tascosa, you were goin' to say?" said Galt tensely.

"What's she got to do with you bein' Galt Magrath? You never saw the Rose of Tascosa, if you're Galt Magrath."

"What makes you so plumb certain of that, mister?" Galt's brain was getting clearer.

"Because I saw her yesterday evenin' near Dodge. I ride with the Rose of Tascosa. I know you never met her."

"Is your name a secret?"

"A man's name is his own business. Sometimes he changes it. I've been called a lot of names. Some of 'em hard 'uns. . . . Here's your gun, Galt Magrath. Shove it back where it won't hurt nobody. Better

163

make sure it's loaded though. I didn't look at it close. Then sit down and take it easy while I build up a fire. We kin auger later, after we're thawed out and feelin' better. But before we make a blaze, I'm takin' a look around. I found only one horse out yonder. Yours, I reckon. And stumbled on you lyin' here by the fire. I took you for dead. Who shot you?"

"I don't know. I had a snake called Windy, from the Mill Iron, and two other gents covered. Then I reckon somebody shot me through the window. Creased me. Left me for dead."

"Was it Pecos Moss?"

"Not knowin', couldn't say. I don't even know if I was shot or hit over the head. What makes you think it was Pecos Moss?"

"I was trailin' him. He was headed in this direction. Lost him in the storm. I'm takin' another look around outside."

"I'll go along. I'm obliged for my gun. As long as you know who I am, and didn't kill me, I reckon I can count on you as a friend."

"That's somethin' I kin promise no man. I claim no man's friendship. I learned that lesson from the Rose of Tascosa. You won't find it in the Bible."

The soft drawl was tainted now with bitterness. Galt followed him out of the cabin.

In the night he looked big. His movements were smooth, quick, and when they had ended their fruitless search for lurking enemies and had kindled a fire, Galt was not surprised to see a tall, splendidly proportioned man. He had straw-colored, straight hair that was graying at the temples, a mustache that was of a darker hue, a bronzed, square-jawed face, and cold, blue-gray eyes that lighted up when he grinned.

"Tex will do for a handle, Galt," he grinned. "It's a moniker that takes in plenty territory. I can't tell you how much because I make a practice of keepin' my mouth shut. But I'll let you know this much. I hate the guts of Pecos Moss. And before he's much older, I'm takin' Lon Coulter to the damnedest whuppin' a man ever got. Which reminds me of somethin' I was goin' to ask you. Lon Coulter claims you and Hipshot killed Jeff Curtis. How about it?"

"As near as Hipshot and I could figure out, Lon Coulter had us both tied to our saddle horns about the time Pecos Moss and some of his men killed Jeff Curtis. We'd taken some Mill Iron horses away from Pecos and two other gents. Set 'em afoot with one horse between 'em, and the last we saw of 'em, they was headed to'rd Las Vegas, one a-ridin, two of 'em goin' by hand. Sort of ride and tie travelin'. Then Pecos showed up in Dodge. I saw him plain. And saw the horse plain, that he was forkin'. And I'd swear by this Bible that he was ridin' a blue roan I'd seen Jeff Curtis ridin' in Las Vegas. The horse he was probably ridin' when he was bushwhacked and killed."

The man who called himself Tex nodded. "Pecos always was stuck on that Blue Dog horse."

"Hipshot and I never killed Jeff Curtis," said Galt hotly, remembering Nancy's uncalled for condemnation. He wasn't actually addressing his companion at all. His tone was vehement.

"I ain't accusin' you," grinned the man, and Galt nodded, scowling at the fire. "There's plenty of men like myself that don't take Lon Coulter's word for it."

"And there's others that do," said Galt.

"For instance?"

"Jeff Curtis's daughter, for one," blurted Galt. He hadn't meant to say that at all. He'd been staring into the fire, musing aloud, hardly aware of the presence of the man. Realization of what he had unintentionally let slip, like some pouting schoolboy, he later told himself, jerked his head up to look at the man.

The cowboy had taken off his shirt and undershirt. And he was working at some bloodstained bandages that bound his ribs and his left arm and shoulder. But his blue-gray eyes, cold, appraising, yet crinkled humorously at the corners, were on Galt, studying him. Galt's face felt hot under the scrutiny.

"Lend me a hand with these bandages, Galt," he said carelessly. "The sawbones at Dodge did a good job but the ridin' in the rain loosened 'em some. Some of Pecos's bushwhackers shot me up a while back. They come damn near gettin' me. Nicked my ribs and hit me in the arm and one bullet tore the chest muscle some. Not a bone broke, though. . . . Just fasten that knot tighter behind my back, will you?"

Then as Galt worked with the bandage, the cowboy went on talking.

"The sawbones was tellin' me about you whuppin' that barber and now they got to callin' you Gospel Galt. And that you was sort of ridin' herd on Jeff's daughter. Now I don't reckon that Nancy Curtis is believin' all that her purty cousin Lon is tellin'. I haven't seen the young 'un for a couple or three years but unless she's changed, she ain't takin' Lon Coulter's say-so for more than it's worth. She's a heady youngster.

Don't let it worry you, young feller. . . . Put the knot tight. I got a hard ride to make. Cattle to gather. And a man to trail down. You got ary special plans in mind?"

"I'm ridin' to Tascosa to find Hipshot. He's poolin' his bets with the Rose of Tascosa."

"The hell he is! Old Hipshot? You're plumb certain?"

"Plumb certain. And as near as I can find out, she's takin' delivery on the cattle and horses that belonged to Jeff Curtis. Pecos Moss is stealin' the herd and remuda and peddlin' the layout to her. But I reckon you know about that?"

The man grinned and nodded. "How'd you like to take a stack of chips in the game?"

"I'm your huckleberry," said Galt.

"The storm has mebbyso throwed a monkey wrench into the machinery. That herd is goin' to be scattered bad. And rustlers are thicker than fleas on a dog. There'll be hard ridin' to do. And some fightin', no doubt. But the Rose of Tascosa pays top wages. Though she don't need to. She's the kind of a woman that men go through hell for her smile."

And Galt, covertly watching the man's face as he spoke, was more than ever convinced of his first guess. That the man who called himself Tex must be Frank Curtis. . . .

Mill Iron cattle in the Lazy J road iron were badly scattered. The storm had struck the Cimarron country with its full, terrific force. It would have taken a small army of cowhands to hold that herd together.

"There's no sense in gettin' excited about it, Galt," said his companion as they rode away from the sod cabin into the dawn. "Let the rustlers like Pecos Moss gather what they kin find. And let Pecos fight the other curly wolves for what they gather. And when they've done all the hardest work of gatherin' them dogies, us boys will step in and take 'em. Lon Coulter and the Mill Iron cowboys will be workin' the country, likewise. I'm right curious to see how him and Pecos will make out. It'll be worth watchin'. Some claim that Lon is scared of Pecos. But I've seen Lon put up some wicked fights. For all his conniverin' ways and his swaggerin' and spur draggin' around town, Lon's game in a tight. And he's dangerous. If he thinks he can't kill a man fair, he'll outfox him and down him from the bush. And so will Pecos. Only Pecos is a better fox than Lon. But I reckon Hipshot wised you up to them two."

Galt nodded, smiling to himself. If this

man was wild Frank Curtis, and Galt was convinced by now that he was, then he was far more dangerous and perhaps as treacherous as either Lon Coulter or Pecos Moss. Windy had accused Frank Curtis of the killing of Preacher Sam. But Galt couldn't picture this big, hard-eyed, easy-grinning man as shooting an unarmed circuit rider in the back.

He was tempted to call the man's hand. Accuse him outright of being Frank Curtis and asking him point-blank what he knew of the murder of Preacher Sam. But Galt was learning caution. He was playing poker. And when you play good poker you don't tip your hand. You hold aces and act like you'd drawn to a bobtail flush and missed. You checked the bet to the other man. You watched him and waited for any mistake he might make. You didn't blurt out things like a bald-faced kid. You kept your hand near your gun and you watched. Galt was too eaten by curiosity not to follow one line of questioning, however.

"That Windy gent was talking about the Rose of Tascosa when I slipped up to the sod cabin and listened outside the window. He gave her a mighty bad rep. And he claimed that she was my mother."

"Listen here, young feller," came the

quick reply, "don't let any damned, forked-tongued snake say a word against the Rose of Tascosa. Kill 'em if they do. And you'll be killin' a liar. A finer, cleaner, straighter woman never lived. And if she is your mother, Galt, be almighty proud of it. Prouder of her than of your sky-pilot father. Because if ever there lived an angel on earth, it's her. If ever you say a word against her, so help me God, I'll kill you as quick as I'd kill a snake."

"That's exactly the way I felt towards that Windy, and the two others that were talkin' about her. I've never killed a man. But I was goin' to kill them three before they could dirty her name any more. I don't remember much about my mother. But if the Rose of Tascosa is her, then I don't reckon you need to worry about havin' to kill me, mister, for turnin' against her in any way. I hated my father for many years for the way he treated her. Knowin' that the Rose of Tascosa is my mother is kind of a shock. But no matter what name she wears now or what they call her, she's my own mother. I'd be proud to claim her and fight for her."

"The Rose of Tascosa," said the man, "will be mighty proud to claim you, Galt. Bible and all."

And Galt knew now, beyond all doubt,

that the Rose of Tascosa was his mother. And that this wide-shouldered man, with the cold, gray-blue eyes and easy grin, was Frank Curtis.

Which made him the uncle of Nancy Curtis. And called for another line of questioning.

"The Mill Iron cattle in the Lazy J road iron belonged to Jeff Curtis, personal," he ventured.

"So I've heard. You're plumb positive?"

"Nancy told me, herself. And now that Jeff Curtis is dead, the cattle and horses belong to her."

"And to nobody else, son." He grinned widely at Galt and slapped him between the shoulders.

"Hell," he added, "what cattle we gather will be turned over to Nancy. You're workin' for the Rose of Tascosa. Not for Pecos Moss."

"Nancy's mighty young to be left alone in Dodge," said Galt. He remembered that Hipshot had said Frank Curtis thought a lot of his little niece and that if he was in Dodge, he'd go see her, regardless.

"She ain't exactly alone, Galt. Aunt Cloe is with her. And Bat Masterson will see to it that nobody harms a hair of her head. Bat and Jeff Curtis were close friends. And personally, I'd as soon face Bat and a dozen deputies as to go against Aunt Cloe when she's on the prod." He chuckled softly, reminiscently.

Galt told about the Negro mammy fainting because of the two dead men being brought up to the Snake Room.

"While Hipshot fed her strong toddies, I read to her from the Bible. She had me readin' till I was hoarse as a crow. She was full of rye whiskey and religion when she finally dropped off to sleep."

"She taken to you and your Bible, I bet," chuckled the big cowboy.

"Even fed me cookies and doughnuts," grinned Galt.

"Then you don't need to bother your head about Lon Coulter makin' his lies stick. I'd rather have Aunt Cloe on my side than the U.S. Cavalry. She won't let you git the worst of it while she's around to take your part. It ain't like Nancy to take anybody's word against a friend, either. Just what happened, if it ain't askin' too personal a question?"

Galt told him how she had openly sided with Lon, there at the cemetery and how he and Hipshot had to run for it and that the Rose of Tascosa had covered their hasty flight.

"Wonder what bit the young 'un. It ain't like her. She's as loyal as a terrier pup." There was a twinkle in his hard eyes when he broke the silence that followed.

"Bet a spotted pony there's another female in it, somewheres." And chuckled when Galt flushed.

By sundown they were as old friends. And Galt found his companion good company. He had an infectious grin and his yarns of the border gave Galt a hint of his reckless, devil-be-damned nature. He laughed a lot, though his steel-colored eyes seldom softened.

And it was at Tascosa the following night that Galt was given proof of the man's cold nerve and courage.

X

Tascosa in the moonlight. Squat, sun-baked adobes with yellow blobs of light showing through the windows. Dusty streets. A plaza about a hundred feet square. In the moonlight and patches of shadow lurked danger and they rode with their hands near their guns. They had waited until dark to enter the little town that had such a wicked reputation. And at a house on the edge of town Galt's companion had made inquiries in a low tone to a Mexican woman who answered his knock at the door of the adobe house. When he mounted his horse again and joined Galt, he grinned faintly.

"Hipshot is with the Rose of Tascosa. But they're not in town. And ain't likely to be, as the outfit pulled out with a mess wagon and bed wagon and horse cavvy. To gather the spilled cattle. The storm stampeded the herd and part of the remuda got away from them Lon Coulter men. No sign of Pecos Moss. But Lon Coulter and a bunch of men was in town to-day. The Señora thinks that Hipshot might be hidin' in town somewhere. It's her job and her old man's job to keep an eye on things. Remember this place if you git in a tight. There's fresh horses in this barn." They pulled up in the shadow of a barn and corral. And a few minutes later were mounted on fresh horses.

"We'll take a look around the saloons before we go back to the Señora's and tie into some real Mexican grub. Might be we'll cut Hipshot's sign. For certain reasons, Galt, I don't want anybody in Tascosa to see me. I'll stay back in the shadow, handy, while you look in the booze joints. And keep your eyes peeled for any of the Pecos Moss gang or the Mill Iron cowhands that might have a horn drooped. Walk careful. I'll be back in the shadow."

They did not ride directly into the plaza but halted alongside one of the saloons. Here Galt dismounted and with his hand on his gun, rounded the corner of the adobe building. And found himself plainly revealed in the light that came from the open doorway. Just as three men rode up.

The light from the saloon temporarily

half-blinded Galt. So that, for a moment, he could not make out the faces of the three riders as they slid their horses to a halt.

A hoarse shout from one of them. Then Galt was suddenly jerked back into the shadow with such force that he fell backwards. And the big man who had handled him so roughly was crouched, half revealed in the light. And the six-shooter in his hand was spewing fire at the three men whose shots had barely missed Galt.

Before Galt could scramble to his feet the fight was over. Three riderless horses milled near the long hitchrack. Their owners lay in the swirling dust kicked up by shod hoofs. And the big cowboy whose swift action had undoubtedly saved Galt from being riddled with bullets, shot again at one of the three men on the ground who had tried to rise. The man went down on his face in the dirt and lay as motionless as the other two. The big cowboy who had been Galt's companion the past twenty-four hours or more, stepped back into the deep shadow, deftly ejecting empty shells from his gun and reloading.

"I don't reckon, Galt," he said, his white teeth showing in a grin that matched the glitter of his steel-colored eyes, "that Windy and his two *compadres* will ever again blacken the name of the Rose of Tascosa. . . .

Let's git out of here."

Then Galt sighted Hipshot coming out of an unlighted adobe, a gun in his hand. Hipshot stood crouched, his back to the adobe wall of the little building, hat slanted across his eyes, his gun ready. As men came piling out of lighted doorways of the saloons.

Galt hailed the old range tramp, for he stood not thirty feet from where Galt and his companion were now back with their horses. Hipshot gave a start, then slid along in the shadows and joined them. He still had his gun in his hand and now it covered Galt's companion.

"Long time no see you, Frank," he said softly, his tone deadly. "Fill your hand."

Galt stepped between them and took Hipshot's gun by the barrel, pushing it downward towards the ground.

"Don't be a fool, Hipshot. Frank Curtis is . . ."

"Shhh," hissed the big cowboy. "Meet me at the Señora's, Hipshot, and whatever's between us kin be settled there. We're wastin' time here."

"Everything's all right," added Galt in a whisper. "I'll be there with Frank, Hipshot. No gun plays."

As Galt and Frank Curtis rode away at a run, Hipshot ducked into the shadows and got his horse, leading the animal from a shed back of the store. He was swearing softly to himself, scowling till his shaggy brows met above his large nose. And when he entered the house where Galt and Frank Curtis waited in a candle-lit back room, he had his hand on his gun and his puckered blue eyes were glittering.

"Put up your gun, Hipshot," said Galt.

"You keep out of this," snapped Hipshot. "Go on out in the kitchen and wait for me there. I got a few words to say to this son of a snake private. Clear out."

"Damned if I will," said Galt. "Only for Frank Curtis I'd be as dead as the three men that tried to fill me full of lead. Hipshot, you're the best friend I have in the world. And I'm not goin' to have you two tangle in a gun argument. I know that the Rose of Tascosa is my mother. And I know that —"

"Do you know that Frank Curtis killed Preacher Sam?" snapped old Hipshot.

"So that's it. If he did, then the job of squarin' the debt belongs to Preacher Sam's son," said Galt. "When Frank tells me he shot an unarmed sky-pilot in the back, I'll not even then take his word for it. Any more than he believes you and I killed his brother Jeff."

"Who told you I killed Preacher Sam,

Hipshot?" asked Frank Curtis.

"I've knowed it all along. Preacher Sam knowed you was gunnin' for him. And he wondered why. He talked it over with me. He said he'd find you and learn the reason. Neither of us had ever sighted the Rose of Tascosa. And we was both too blind and dumb to put two and two together and tally the natural score. I wouldn't hold it against you, then or now, if you'd killed an armed man in a fair fight. You'd sent word to Preacher Sam to swap his Bible for a gun and learn to use it. You might have knowed he wouldn't pack a gun. But you was willin' to turn coward and murderer to make the woman you loved a widder so she could marry you. She loved you. But while Preacher Sam lived, you couldn't belong to one another. And she was a good woman. She wouldn't give herself even to the one man she loved, till she was married to him, legal. And she knowed that Preacher Sam would never give her a divorce because he was stricter than the pope in Rome regardin' divorces.

"I ain't askin' you if you killed Preacher Sam. I read the sign around where he was killed. And checked up close on you. But I ain't askin' you that question that Galt here mentioned. But I'm tellin' you and Galt this. That the reason you ain't married right now to the Rose of Tascosa is because she knows you killed Preacher Sam.

"Preacher Sam was as close to me as a blood brother, mister. He was murdered. I swore by his dead body that I'd square his debt. Galt, git out of the room. The only answer Frank Curtis has is in his gun leather."

Then the closed door behind old Hipshot opened. The hinges creaked a little. And in the doorway stood a copper-haired woman in fringed, shabby buckskin. But she was not looking at Hipshot or Frank Curtis. Her eyes, dark with emotion, were looking at Galt.

For a moment Galt stared at her, the color drained from his face. Then with a choked cry he crossed the little room and gathered her swaying form in his arms.

Frank Curtis looked at Hipshot and slipped out the door. Hipshot followed, closing the door behind him on the mother and son.

They had no need of words to bridge the long gap of the years that were behind them. Because there was too much to say that could not be told in words. And even as they clung to one another and the tears of this woman, who had forgotten how to weep, were wetting the rough, unshaved cheek of this man who was her son, each of them knew that there would always be an invisible barrier between them. A barrier of silence that could make for a greater love or a lasting strangeness and misunderstanding. Because Mary Magrath, who had become the Rose of Tascosa, had been marked for life. By those years since her small son had been torn from her arms one night, a long time ago, in a dingy hotel room at Dodge City.

If anything, she was more beautiful than ever. Age did not mar her face with lines and her figure was young and lithe. No threads of silver showed in her thick mass of coppery hair. She was the most beautiful woman Galt had ever seen.

But the softness of her was gone. Gone from her smile and her eyes. In its place was character and strength. Tolerance was there, beneath, and perhaps pity. But Preacher Sam had killed the sweet softness of her youth and girlhood. Killed it with a stern brutality he had mistaken for justice and something else that belonged to God and was too great and too delicate an instrument for human handling. If there was hardness in this woman they called the Rose of Tascosa, then Galt's father had been its cause. Galt knew that, somehow. And tightened his arms around her. And for those brief moments she forgot that he was Preacher Sam's flesh and blood and claimed him as hers solely.

Her hands, trembling a little, stroked his cheek that was rough with a stubble of beard. They fingered his thick hair that was matted with sweat and dust. And her eyes were shut, her face pressed against his dusty flannel-clad shoulder. Neither of them spoke. They stood there for a long time like that. There was something desperately pathetic about the way they clung to one another. In Galt's heart was nothing but love and pity and understanding for his mother. He knew that she hated the memory of his father. And Hipshot had told him, more than once, that he bore a striking resemblance to Preacher Sam. Of course, the sight of him must be tearing her heart. She must be fighting a hatred for him because he was so much like Preacher Sam in appearance. Galt understood and felt all the more pity for her.

Then the buckskin-covered Bible, with its lasting stains of Preacher Sam's blood on it, dropped from Galt's pocket and fell to the floor between them. Was it some prophetic symbol? For they loosed their embrace and Galt stooped and picked the Bible up from the hard-packed dirt floor. He stood with it in his hand, awkwardly. And stared dumbly at the look of loathing and hatred that hardened his mother's gray eyes. And then her eyes traveled upward from that buckskin-covered Bible she had recognized, to the face of her stalwart son. The son who so strongly resembled his father. And it was as if she forgot that he was her son and was looking at Preacher Sam.

"Gospel Galt!" she spat the name at him. "Preaching sermons from that damned book! Singing hypocrite psalms and smashing lives of helpless fools that believe in something called religion. Take your precious Bible and get out of Tascosa. Get out of my sight. When you've thrown that thing away, come back."

She whirled on her heels, silver-mounted spurs jingling. She was gone before Galt, stunned as if slapped across the mouth, could call out. He heard the pounding of shod hoofs outside as she rode away. He was still standing there, the buckskin-covered Bible in his hands, when old Hipshot came into the room.

"Come on, son," he said in a colorless tone, taking Galt's arm, and leading him towards the door. "Time we was movin' along."

Hipshot and Galt rode for some time in silence. Then the old range tramp spoke.

"I got me an outfit together. Some of the fastest cowhands that ever wet the hide of a Mexican dogie in the Rio Grande. A few of the Mill Iron boys that didn't swaller Lon Coulter's lies. Some more that was plumb disgusted with the ways of Pecos Moss. We got the bulk of the remuda they spilled, and the mess wagon and bed wagon with its grub and a keg of likker that Pecos Moss outfitted here in Tascosa. We're fixed to go into the cattle business for ourselves. That storm has spilled all kinds of cattle all over the landscape and the pickin's is like a rustler's dream come true. Son, you and me has bin roundsidin' too much around town. Gittin' too soft. What we need is plenty good hard cattle work. I'm ramroddin' the fastest, toughest outfit between Mexico and the Canadian line. You're tophand and bookkeeper. In a week we'll have a gatherment of longhorns that you'll have to raise rifle sights to shoot acrost. Here. Take a drink. You look like a sick calf. Good likker and hard ridin' never killed no man yet. It's this roundsidin' in town that throws yuh."

Galt took a small drink. "What happened between you and Frank Curtis?" he asked.

"We come to a workin' agreement. He went with *her*."

XI

Dust and sun and the bawling of cattle. Long hours in the saddle. Night guarding the stuff they gathered. Riding long circles that began before real daylight. Working big herds. Forgetting to wash the dirt and sweat from their bodies but never neglecting to keep their guns free from clogging dust. Hard work. Dangerous work. Hardly a day passed that Hipshot's men did not exchange shots with other riders.

For the freak storm, the worst in years, had scattered several trail herds and had drifted other cattle from the range of big and small outfits in that strip of country. So that reps from several big spreads were working with Hipshot's men.

Galt was riding a string of the best horses he had ever forked. And even old Hipshot admitted that he was better than the average tophand. And the reps from the other out-fits respected his honesty. This was more than a compliment in that part of the country where rustling prevailed.

A big man with iron-gray beard and thick hair rode up with half a dozen men as Hip-shot and his cowhands drove bunches of the cattle they had gathered to the hold-up ground a mile or so from the round-up camp on the Canadian.

"The old gent with the whiskers," Hip-shot said to Galt, "is the cattle king of this part of the country. And his opinion of me won't stand testin'. I'll ride out and talk to him. You stay here at the herd."

"Like hell," grinned Galt. "We've been treatin' him and his cattle right and if he don't know it, it's time he found out. I'll talk to him."

"He was raised on whiskey and raw lion-meat. He's tough. You kin hear him beller fer miles and when he paws the earth you can't see the sun for the dust."

But Galt grinned and rode on to meet the formidable cowman with the whiskers. Hip-shot, his hand on his six-shooter, tightened his jaws and rode alongside him.

"Who's roddin' this rustler spread?" bel-lowed the big cowman, and his beard seemed to bristle.

"It's not a rustler outfit," Galt spoke up. "I reckon you know that. We've gathered over two hundred head of your strays. I got a tally of everything in your iron that was gathered . . . and turned back onto your range. If that's rustlin', there ain't any such thing as an honest cow outfit."

"Hmm. Young roosters crow the loudest. Looks like ol' Hipshot's got lockjaw and is tongue-tied. Will you explain just what right you got to be workin' this range? Do you or Hipshot own ary cattle that gives you the right to work my country for strays? Answer me that, young button."

"You can be almighty thankful, sir, that it's our outfit and not Pecos Moss or one of the other layouts that's workin' this range that don't belong to you or any other outfit. I told you what we did with the cattle in your brand that we gathered. You knew all about it before you rode here. We're not exactly short-handed, sir, but if you wanted to drop a man or two with the outfit, we'll be proud to have 'em with us."

The old cowman snorted into his beard and his hard eyes glittered in the sunlight.

"By God, young rooster, you'll do. I fetched along six of my men. All tophands. Their horses will be here by sundown. You'll do. Hipshot, is this the young sky-pilot feller they call Gospel Galt?"

"It is," said old Hipshot, speaking for the first time, "and you sized him up right. He'll do to take along. You knowed his father. Preacher Sam."

"I did. And I didn't like his damned fire and brimstone hollerin'. Told him to git off my range and stay off. If my boys needed religion they could ride to town an' git it with their whiskey and poker. Bible spoutin' is all right in its place. But not around cow camps. What's this about you stealin' them wagons at Tascosa and mountin' your men on Mill Iron horses, Hipshot?"

"The cook that was drivin' the mess wagon and the swamper that was drivin' the bed wagon got drunk in Tascosa and kind of lost their bearin's. And forgot who they was hired out to. I taken pity on 'em, you might say, and let 'em trail along with me. And them Mill Iron ponies belong to Jeff Curtis's daughter. She kin have 'em when she comes for 'em. We're just keepin' 'em safe for the young 'un. The boys ride 'em just to keep 'em sort of gentled."

"They accuse you and young Gospel here of murderin' Jeff."

"You believe that?"

"If I did, I'd kill you where you set your horse right now. I'm sendin' over about sixty head of extra horses with the strings that belong to these six boys. Figgered you might need 'em. And you kin send your mess wagon to my ranch for grub when you need it. Hipshot, I know you've run off my cattle from time to time, durin' past years. And I swore I'd make it hot for you when I cut your sign. I ain't trustin' you fu'ther than out of gun range, even now. I'm a hard man. I'm not softenin' up none now. What I'm doin' is gamblin' on this young Gospel feller. I've heard some stories about him that tickled me. Bat Masterson told me quite a bit when he was at my ranch a week ago. He told me how the young button here had whupped that barber called Sport McAllister. I'd give a hundred head of fat steers to have seen it. I dozed off once in the barber chair and that damned pinhead trimmed my eyebrows. By God, he did! Only I didn't know it till I got back to the ranch. Otherwise I'd have killed the perfume stinkin', lily fingered, pinheaded son of a monkey."

Hipshot struggled with a grin at the old cattleman's wrathy remembrance of the incident that is one of the sagas of the cattle trails. And as Bat Masterson afterwards claimed, it was the barber-whipping incident and little else that first interested the cattle king of the Cimarron and Canadian in Galt Magrath whom he always afterwards called Gospel.

Now he fixed his cold, penetrating eye on Hipshot once more. And leaned a little closer, gnarled hands on his saddle horn.

"What's this SS iron you're runnin' on some of the strays you're gatherin' and holdin' along with all Mill Iron stuff that's in the Lazy J road iron?"

"It's a brand I'm puttin' on every critter I find that was in that San Saba Pool herd that was run off by rustlers and sold. But as Galt says, I reckon you already knowed without askin' that question."

"Gospel here said I'd know?"

"I told Hipshot you'd like as not agree with our idea since you was one of the cattlemen who wouldn't buy any of that San Saba Pool stuff from the rustlers. You see we aim to sell the SS cattle we gather and divide the proceeds among the widows and children left behind by the San Saba Pool men that got massacred on the Staked Plains."

"The hell you say. That's puttin' your Bible teachin' into good practice, Gospel. That's the kind of religion any honest man kin savvy without havin' Bible school learnin'. That's where you differ from Preacher Sam. You'll do, Gospel. You'll do."

"It was Galt's idee," admitted Hipshot. "I aimed to git the cattle all right, but the rest of the idee belongs to Galt. You're plumb right, mister, about Galt. He'll do."

Old Hipshot winked. "There's a drop or two left in the keg, Spud, if you'll ride to camp with me."

You didn't call the cattle king of the Cimarron and Canadian range "Spud" unless you knew him mighty well. Pat Dulin had knocked men down for undue familiarity. And behind the nickname Spud was a story that had to do with his being so poor when he started in the cattle business that he fed the one cowhand he could then afford on nothing but potatoes he grew on his ranch and maverick beef. So Pat Dulin gained the name Spud and secretly gloried in it and all that lay behind it.

"I could do with a drop, Hipshot," he snorted, and they rode off together towards camp. One of the PD cowpunchers grinned widely at Galt.

"Looks like the old man taken a likin' to you, button. If he has, you're the luckiest cowhand that ever come up the trail. If that old son likes you he'll go through hell for you. But if he don't, he'll make that hot stretch of country called the Hornada look ice cold compared to the ground under your feet. He'll run you so far out of the country you'll be dead of old age by the time you quit travelin'."

"When you shoved Sport McAllister's head in the water barrel," agreed a second PD cowhand, "you just nacherally moved in on an interest in the PD outfit. The old man considered the barber too harmless a thing to kill. And he's laid awake of a night tryin' to scheme out a way of gittin' even with that hair-tonic mixer for whittlin' on his eyebrows."

"And you was right about him bein' wise to what was goin' on at this layout of Hipshot's. We've bin watchin' you since you commenced work a week or two ago. There ain't much that Spud Dulin misses. You treated him square and he's as tickled as a kid with his first pair of red-topped, brass-toed boots. The old man's tough and he's a scrapper. But he's honest, so far as the cattlemen kin be called plumb honest. And he's hell on rustlers."

"I've heard him cuss Hipshot for a rustler."

"Hipshot? Hell, that old range tramp likes to make out he's the worst rustler either side of the Pecos. I know better. How about it, Gospel?"

Galt winced a little at the name. But

Dodge City had branded it on him and it was there to stay. He grinned and nodded.

"They don't come any finer than Hipshot. I know." And his eyes followed the backs of Hipshot and Spud Dulin who were riding slowly towards camp, talking earnestly.

Galt was glad to know that this PD cowhand saw through old Hipshot's sham and pretense at being a no-account old renegade. And he reckoned that Spud Dulin had also penetrated the grizzled range tramp's disguise and saw the real man beneath.

But nobody could ever know the splendid loyalty of Hipshot as Galt had found it since that day when he fetched the bloodstained, buckskin-covered Bible and news of Preacher Sam's death to the boy. Hipshot had gone beyond the limits of mere friendship. In his own unobtrusive way he had been Galt's teacher, his guide, his pardner in time of need. Times when Galt had felt that fate or God or whatever it was in life that shaped things for men, had given him a shabby deal, it had been Hipshot's quaint philosophy that had made him believe again.

When the Rose of Tascosa had so turned against him, and Galt had been more deeply hurt than ever before in his life, Hipshot hadn't even talked about it for several days.

194

Instead he had thrown Galt into so much hard, dangerous work that the young cowpuncher hadn't time to worry or grieve. And only after the worst of the hurt was gone and the pain in his heart had dulled, only then did Hipshot bring up the delicate subject. Waiting until one night on guard when they rode together around the bedded cattle. Then the old range tramp had talked. And in the end Galt had understood things and Hipshot had acted as if the boy had understood all along and that they were just discussing it as if Galt hadn't been hurt at all. And that they felt sorry for her and would scheme around somehow to make her happy and make up for the way Preacher Sam had treated her.

"You should have seen her that night at Dodge when you talked there by that grave. I was watchin' and wonderin' how she'd act. I'd lay a bet that she kin almost repeat, word for word, what you said that night. Of course she lets on that she don't even believe in God. But the girls at Dodge and Tascosa will tell a different story. She's done more good amongst them pore things than all the sky-pilots in the world. So the other night when you'd bedded down I slipped off and rode to Tascosa and seen her. And when I done finished talkin' to her she was laughin'. You and her need one another. But right now it's better that you don't meet for a while. You bein' the spittin' image of Preacher Sam kinda stirs her up. I told her I'd have you grow a set of pink whiskers and wear a patch over one eye and stutter when you talked broken American like a Swede. And while I had her with her guard dropped and in a good humor, I borrowed the loan of three of her top cowhands. They'll be over with us to-morrow." And old Hipshot had chuckled to himself.

That was the kind of a man old Hipshot was. And men like Spud Dulin and Bat Masterson saw through the old rascal's shamming. So did this PD cowboy and Galt reckoned that other men felt the same way about the range tramp who preferred a drifting, aimless life to any one of several ramrod jobs he could have had for the asking. Hipshot was now proving that he was as expert a wagon-boss as ever handled men in a tight.

It must have been an hour before Hipshot and Spud Dulin left camp. The cattle king headed for his home ranch. Hipshot showed up at the herd a trifle tipsy and with a grin on his seamed, leathery face.

"Spud's sendin' me over a keg. You know, son, it wouldn't surprise me none if, some day, all these cowhands you see around this herd that's still alive, will be takin' orders from you. The old man's just nacherally adopted you. How's chances for a cushy job in my old age around the PD ranch?"

Of course Hipshot was only joshing but had he known what was going on in the mind of that bellowing, rough-spoken old cattleman he would not have been greatly surprised. Because Hipshot, for all his careless ways, was a shrewd judge of men. And he knew that Galt had somehow touched a tender spot beneath the hard exterior of old Spud Dulin. . . .

To get a quicker work of the country, Hipshot split the outfit in two. He put Galt in charge of the men who would work north of the Canadian towards the Cimarron. While he took a pack outfit and the other cowhands and drifted towards the Red River.

"You'll take the PD men and the Mill Iron cowboys that quit Lon Coulter and come with us. I'm takin' the men that the Rose of Tascosa sent to rep with us, and the deserters from the Pecos Moss spread. They're all curly wolves and I'm takin' 'em on a little pasear into the strip where the rustlers hang out."

Reps from several other outfits joined Galt's spread the second day of the work.

Galt sized them up with a tightening of his jaw muscles. He didn't quite like the looks of some of the new men. In his travels with Hipshot he had cut the trail of two or three of them and knew that they had ridden with Pecos Moss, from time to time. He looked for trouble and said so to the PD men and the Mill Iron cowboys.

"There's two men repping for the Lazy 8," he summed up the newcomers. "Two more representin' the YT iron. And three that claim to be reppin' for what they call the Two Pole Pumpkin iron. The Lazy 8 and the YT both bought a lot of the stolen San Saba Pool cattle from Pecos Moss. And take a look at this."

Squatting on his heels, he leveled a space in the dirt with the palm of his hand. Then with a stick he made the Mill Iron brand.

"Now watch the Mill Iron get changed into the Two Pole Pumpkin."

And with the pointed stick he changed the Mill Iron $\subset$ into the Two Pole Pumpkin Θ.

He grinned faintly at the Mill Iron men. "I don't need to tell you boys that when Lon Coulter helped Jeff Curtis run the Lazy J road iron on the Mill Iron stuff Jeff bought back on the San Saba, he did a neat job of brandin'. A lot of the brands he put on never peeled because the iron never bit into the hide. Only burned the hair and scorched the hide. That's why Hipshot ordered every critter we rounded up that was in the Lazy J road iron to be branded over if the brand didn't show plain. And we've re-branded nearly a hundred head that had haired over already so much that you couldn't hardly make out the dim brand."

"Jeff jumped Lon about it," said a Mill Iron man, "before he pulled out for Las Vegas. And told Lon to re-brand everything that wasn't branded right, as soon as he reached the Canadian where you and Hipshot found us camped when Lon fetched you there, prisoners. Jeff give Lon hell about it. I heard him. But Lon never re-branded anything."

"Who owns the Two Pole Pumpkin iron?" Galt asked a PD man.

"Pecos Moss, so far as Spud could find out."

"In the mornin'," said Galt, "we're makin' a long circle. Gather everything in the Two Pole Pumpkin, the Lazy 8 and the YT iron that you can find. We're claimin' 'em."

"That'll call for fightin', Gospel."

"Any man that didn't hire out for a tough hand can pull out of the game."

"We'll stand at your back till your belly caves in, Gospel."

"Then ketch out your circle horses in the mornin' and blow the cobwebs out of your gun barrels."

So mid-morning the next day found Galt lazing in his saddle on a little knoll watching the cattle being driven from all compass points to the hold-up ground. Long strings of cattle flanked by riders. Dust against the sun. The bawling of cattle. A cloudless blue sky overhead. The tune of an old cowboy trail song threading through the blur of other noises.

This was the life that Galt loved. And even the hardships of it all only added to its fascination. He had been born to it, raised with it, and it was a part of his existence. A born cowboy can never change. Though he may become something else in life, as years go by, he is a cowboy inside his heart and nothing this side of death can change that part of him. Sun and dust. Star-filled nights and lightning storms. Thirst and blizzards. Long hours in the saddle with the ground for a bed and the sky for a roof. Dangers and hardships. A man's lonely life in which women can have but a small part. A cowboy cusses it all and wouldn't trade places with a king on a golden throne.

The song, plaintive, minor-keyed, threaded out of the sun-filtered dust below. . . .

"Bury me not on the lone prairee. . . ."

Before the sun went down that dry prairie soil might be stained with the blood of brave men who would never ride another circle. Perhaps the cowboy who was singing now would never sing again.

Though the day was hot, Galt felt a sort of chill run along his spine and the sun seemed less bright, less yellow in the dust haze. And the sky up above lost something of its blue.

Perhaps Preacher Sam had read often from that passage, for the pages were soiled a little from thumbing and it was a little worn as if the place had been marked by the circuit rider's long, big-knuckled forefinger when he held the Bible closed in his big hand. That passage from Christ's Sermon on the Mount:

"Thou shalt not kill; and whosoever shall kill shall be in danger of the judgment."

Galt closed the Bible with its stained, buckskin cover. He put it back in one of the home-made saddle pockets and buckled down the flap on it. He made certain that his long-barreled six-shooter would slide easily from its old holster. Then he rode down the slope and into the dust haze below. To become a part of it. To take his place among the riders as ramrod of the outfit.

XII

Galt and a grizzled, hard-bitten old Mill Iron cowpuncher whose loyalty to Jeff Curtis had been tried and proven, rode into the herd. For more than half an hour they cut straight Mill Iron cattle marked with a plain Lazy J road iron. And when the last of the straight Mill Iron stuff had been worked out of the herd and they had spent some minutes looking through the herd of mixed brands to make sure they had worked it clean, they rode to the edge of the hold-up to wind their sweating horses. Three men held the "cut" that contained the steers they had cut out. The other riders sat their horses holding the main bunch together.

"That's the size of 'em, Gospel."

Galt nodded. "We'll commence cuttin' the Two Pole Pumpkin stuff. And we'll start with that big black steer with one horn knocked off. Wasn't he a lead steer and marker in the trail herd that belonged to Jeff?"

"He was, Gospel. But the road iron has wore off so it don't show and they done a clumsy job of makin' the Mill Iron into a Two Pole Pun'kin. Even a green hand could tell it's a worked brand. And I seen them Two Pole Pun'kin men sizin' him up and arguin' amongst theirselves. Every man in the outfit, I reckon, has spotted that steer. He was a leader on the way up. We call him Booger."

A PD rep and one of the old Mill Iron hands had been between the hold-up and the cut, keeping tally. Whenever Galt and his team-mate cut a critter from the hold-up they would call out the brand and the two tally men would sing out after him and mark it in their tally books.

Galt and his pardner rode past them and Galt spoke to them in a low-pitched, even tone that was as careless as he could make it.

"We're startin' to whittle out the Pumpkin stuff. . . ."

He and the Mill Iron man rode into the herd. And as if it were some sort of prearranged signal, the cowpunchers who took their orders from him and Hipshot and were loyal, casually maneuvered so as to be handy

when trouble started. They managed to unobtrusively cover the reps from the Lazy 8,
the YT and Two Pole Pumpkin outfits.

Galt cut the Booger steer past the
Pumpkin trio and past the two tally men.
And sang out in a loud voice.

"Mill Iron. Tally him for re-brand into
Lazy J road iron. One of Jeff's. . . . And
there's more a-comin'."

The pick-up men hazed the Booger steer
into the cut. Galt rode up to where the three
Pumpkin reps, flanked by three old Mill
Iron hands, sat their horses.

"You saw the steer I just cut out. You
heard what I told the tally men. I'll make it
plain enough for you three hombres to
savvy. I'm cuttin' all Two Pole Pumpkin
stuff into the Mill Iron herd. This evenin'
you three reps is goin' to ketch every
Pumpkin critter and put it into Jeff
Curtis's Lazy J road iron. Are you takin'
my orders?"

"We'll cut our strings first," said one of
them. "You can't treat us thataway. We're
gittin' the rawest deal ever handed a rep.
Them's Pun'kin steers belongin' to the
outfit we rep for. We ain't puttin' 'em into
no man's road brand."

"Who owns the Two Pole Pumpkin?"
asked Galt.

"Pecos Moss. Pecos Moss and Lon Coulter."

"So Lon Coulter is in on it. That's all I need to know." Galt's six-shooter flashed in the sunlight. Even Bat Masterson would have nodded approval of that swift draw. He thumbed the hammer back.

"See how high you can stretch your arms. Claw for a gun and I'll start shootin'. I ain't foolin'."

"You can't treat us thisaway," growled one of them, lifting his arms. "You can't do this to us."

"Mebby not. Mebby not. But from where I'm sittin' behind this gun, I'd say you was wrong as hell. . . . You know your orders, boys," he said to the Mill Iron men. "Have at 'em."

It took hardly a minute to disarm the three Pumpkin reps and slip a noose over the head of each. So that they sat their horses, each with a saddle rope around his neck. The other ends of the three ropes were dallied around the saddle horns of three Mill Iron cowboys.

"Try to fight the ropes," said Galt, grinning mirthlessly, "and you'll get jerked so damned hard your necks will pop like guns. Remember that while the boys lead you to camp. You'll have a couple of hours to think it over careful about putting these Pumpkin steers into Jeff Curtis's road iron. Take 'em to camp, cowboys. If they fight their lead ropes, go south with 'em."

Galt and his pardner rode back into the hold-up. As they began cutting out Two Pole Pumpkin steers, Galt saw the reps from the Lazy 8 and YT outfits head for camp. Which meant that they were cutting their string of horses and pulling out for home. They had no taste for any of the medicine Gospel Galt was handing out to the Pumpkin reps. They had taken the broad hints dropped them by the PD cowboys.

And in the cool of the evening of that same day the three sullen and beaten Pumpkin reps worked at roping Two Pole Pumpkin steers and branding them with Jeff Curtis's Lazy J road iron. They finished just before dark, caught fresh horses and quit the round-up camp, driving their string of horses into the dusk.

"Spud Dulin hisself," said an old PD hand, "couldn't have made a neater job of it, Gospel. Nary a gun fired off. Sweet as sorghum."

Galt was level-headed enough not to place too high a value on this bloodless victory. There would be plenty of trouble before they got to Dodge with the cattle they gathered. He doubled the night guards and spent half the night in the saddle, scouting around to discover any attempt on the part of the rustlers to "Injun" up on the camp.

"Don't forget what happened to the San Saba Pool men," he repeated. Galt was taking no chances on a surprise attack and stampede. Though he knew that these seasoned hands, all older than himself, needed no cautioning or advice.

"I feel like some smart Aleck school kid givin' advice to his teachers, and tellin' 'em how to run their school," he told them when Hipshot put him in charge of the outfit.

"When we commence to bellyache and cuss you behind your back, Gospel," said a PD man, "then you'll know you've made good. Nacherally, none of us old hands like to take orders from a bald-faced button."

Galt wondered just how much truth was behind that joshing remark. Plenty, he reckoned. And he'd better not make any bad mistakes. He was holding down a job that many an old hand would have hesitated about taking. He was responsible for a clean and careful working of this range. And he had the lives of these men in his hands. Though he was wise enough to know that they'd never let him make a bad blunder. They needed few orders.

Because they were a breed of men not given to handing out praise, their words of approval meant a lot to Galt and he felt elated. But he knew that without their cooperation he would never have been able to get rid of those reps without a gun fight.

It was after the reps had gone and most of the outfit were gathered around the coffeepot, that these older hands were given a little surprise that tickled their fancy.

"What I can't figger out," said an old Mill Iron cowhand, "is why Pecos or them Pun'kin cowboys ever was fool enough to work the brand on that Booger steer. They might have got away with an argument on the other stuff they branded into the Pun'kin iron. But every man in the outfit there knowed that Booger steer. And the changed brand was a dead give-away. It cinched our bets, complete. Left no argument as to what they'd bin doin' to the Mill Iron brand. That Booger steer was a dead give-away."

"That's what I figured," Galt grinned, "when I roped and throwed him and run that Two Pole Pumpkin on his black hide."

"You? You mean, Gospel, that you. . . . Well, I'll be damned!"

It became one of the yarns Spud Dulin was to tell and retell in town and around

round-up camps. The story of the Booger steer.

Somehow, it gave a tang to the bloodless victory that seemed too tame to these veterans of the cattle trails. They had been a little disappointed because there had been no fighting. But this gave a flavor to its flatness and they felt better.

For eight days and nights they worked as hard as ever cowboys had labored. They ran low on grub and tobacco. They averaged less than four hours sleep out of twenty-four. The weather had been tricky. Sultry and then a lightning storm that had kept every man in the saddle all night. Their horses were gaunting up. And the men were touchy and ornery. They growled and snapped at one another like wolves. Twice they flared into swift quarrels that almost ended in gunplay. They cussed Galt and the grub and the weather and the cattle they gathered.

Galt, his lean face covered with dust-grimed whiskers, bloodshot eyes sunken in their sockets, had less sleep than any man. He was always the first to finish a hurried meal and dump his empty plate and cup in the dishpan. Always he was the first man saddled. And if he drove his men hard, he drove himself still harder. And they knew it.

The circles they rode were long. They rode leg-weary horses to camp. Wolfed some grub, saddled a fresh horse, and went back to work the herd and brand stuff into the SS and Lazy J road iron. They moved camp twice a day.

"If you're out to make a rep for yourself as a slave-drivin' ramrod," growled a man, "you're shore a-doin' it. A man don't need a bed to work with this wagon."

"It shore don't take a man long to stay overnight at camp," agreed Galt with a grin. "We're doublin' the guard again to-night. You'll go on third guard."

They were using the fancy stem-winder Hipshot had given Galt for a guard watch. And in order to shorten his guard hour, one of the younger cowpunchers tried the old trick of setting the hands ahead half an hour. But Galt had been expecting the trick and checked the guard watch with the cook's battered old silver watch. And jumped the guilty time thief.

"Ketch a horse and go on bobtail guard," he told the cowboy, without mentioning the fact that he had discovered who had tampered with the stem-winder.

Bobtail guard or killpecker is the shift that goes on at sundown or near that hour and comes off at eight o'clock when the first guard men take over the herd.

"And you'll go on graveyard guard like-wise," finished Galt.

"Killpecker and graveyard the same night? You've pulled the wrong badger out of the hole this time. Mebby it's a joke you read out of your damned Bible."

Galt hadn't meant to let his temper get the upper hand. But his nerves were rubbed raw and mention of the Bible in a sneering tone touched off the needed spark to cause the explosion. His open-handed slap caught the cowboy across the mouth. Then they were fighting.

It was a short, punishing fight. No rules. No holds barred. They gave and took. And for Galt it was a sort of outlet for everything inside him that had been bottled up too tightly. He gave the cowboy a whipping that left him on the ground, bloody and beaten. But one of Galt's eyes was closed and discolored and his nose streamed blood.

"I got enough, Gospel," muttered the cowboy through battered, bleeding lips. "I'll go on bobtail. And I'll stand your damned graveyard guard."

"And from now on one of your guard pardners will tell you the time to go off guard," grinned Galt, his anger gone.

This brought some coarse laughter and

hoorawing from the other hands. And the beaten man got to his feet grinning through the smear of blood and dirt.

"So that was it. You win, Gospel. You never said nothin' about the stem-winder not keepin' correct time."

"You didn't mention the subject."

"I never was good at tellin' time nohow," grinned the guilty cowboy and he went to catch his night horse.

And the men who had been cheated the previous night of half an hour's sleep by the tampering with the stem-winder, called ribald and cutting remarks after the time robber, as he was now called.

Hipshot would have approved of Galt's manner of handling the affair. Because had the men who lost their precious sleep taken up the matter of punishing the offender, it might have ended in gunplay. Because their nerves and tempers were galled raw and it would have taken little to start a free-for-all fight among them. Galt's fists and his grin had done the job. Galt was making good. As Hipshot or Spud Dulin would have said it, he'd do.

But Galt, riding alone that night on his habitual nocturnal scouting, was burdened with worry. A worry he dared not share with any man for fear of injuring their morale.

Hipshot was a day overdue. He and his men should have been camped near here yesterday, with what cattle they had gathered.

Galt tried to convince himself that old Hipshot had been delayed by natural causes, between the Red River and the Canadian. That he'd be along tomorrow with a big herd. But somehow he couldn't believe what he kept telling himself. Something had happened to Hipshot.

"Oh, God, don't let 'em kill Hipshot. . . ." And with the prayer went a silent, sinister promise to himself to avenge with his gun any harm done to his pardner. . . .

Galt eased up on the work the next day. To give his men and horses a chance to rest, he explained carelessly. In reality, it was to keep his part of the plan to meet Hipshot here on the North Fork of the Canadian. He'd lay over until Hipshot got here with his drive from down on the Red. In the bright light of day something of Galt's fear for Hipshot's safety disappeared. He saddled a long-legged circle horse and left camp. While the others augered in the shade and the men on day herd lazed in their saddles as the cattle spread out, grazing.

"I wouldn't stray too far, Gospel," said an old-timer. "Lon Coulter is camped somewhere on the Canadian. He's got some of

Pecos men and a cavvy of horses they picked up here and there. They're not quite afoot and Lon's got a horn drooped. Them Pun'kin reps is with Lon and they ain't forgot the Booger steer. Better not ride alone. Take a couple of us along, why don't you?"

"I'm ridin' a horse that can out-run their bullets. Anyhow, I'm not driftin' far."

He knew about Lon Coulter throwing in with Pecos. And he wondered a lot what Nancy Curtis was thinking by now, back in Dodge City. Frank had told Galt that Bat Masterson would ride herd on her. But that wouldn't keep her from worrying her heart sick. He'd been too proud to send her word that he and Hipshot were working to gather her cattle for her. She'd called him a rustler and believed Lon Coulter's lies about the murder of Jeff. His revenge would come when he delivered her cattle at Dodge. Till then, let her keep on thinking anything she wanted. The worse she damned him, the cheaper she'd feel when he proved her wrong. And he would not admit to himself that he was suffering as much as she was. And that it was taking every shred of his will power to keep from sending her a letter telling her not to worry. That he'd already gathered two-thirds of her cattle and had the bulk of her remuda. As a matter of fact, he'd written more than a couple such messages, then destroyed them the next morning.

He topped a ridge that looked down on the river. And pulled up to look around. But so far as he could see in any direction, there was no sign of Hipshot's outfit coming with a trail herd. He dismounted and loosened his saddle cinch. Then sat down in the shade of his horse. This was as good a spot as any for a lookout. Fairly well screened by brush from any riders, he commanded a good view of the surrounding country.

He sat there, dozing. Then the utter weariness of his tired body got the better of him and in a few minutes he was sound asleep, his back propped against scrub cedar.

It was mid-afternoon when he jerked awake with a start, his hand on his gun. But a quick look around dissipated his fears and he grinned shamefacedly as the sun and the stem-winder told him it was two hours past noon. And then he caught the sounds that had probably wakened him. They came from below, at the river crossing. He saw a team of mules hitched to a covered light spring wagon bogged in the mud. A rider trying to help pull the bogged rig with a saddle rope tied to the wagon tongue and snubbed to the saddle horn. But somehow the mules and saddle horses were not pulling together. It looked like the mules had balked. And the rider, weight in one stirrup, twisted to divide the weight with the pull, called orders to the driver of the mule team.

"When I holler 'Ready,' pour the whip to those long-eared, sheep-brained, balking, overgrown jackrabbits. Throw the buckskin out among 'em and cuss like a mule skinner."

Galt was on his feet as if shot from the ground by a steel spring. And a blank look of astonishment crossed his bearded face. Then he grinned widely, his heart pounding against his ribs. For the rider's voice was not that of a man. It was Nancy Curtis.

And from the canvas-covered wagon showed a black head bound with a red bandanna. And a rich, though weary and plaintive voice called out:

"Bad as 'at hotel was wif its dead co'pses an' its drunk goin's on below, it was lak paradise redeemed, seems to me now. Lawdygawdy, stuck in 'is mud an's sinkin' fast. These heah beast of de devil is jes' nacherally sot down in de mud lak dey enjoy it. Every bone in my po' body bust' an' achin' wid de misery. Flies an' mosquitoes in de air. Snakes an' wolves on de groun'. Injuns a-prowlin' of a night, a-screechin' fo' my po' scalp. Moses, lead us fum 'is heah wildahness! Wha'at is you, Gawd? Save a po' sinnah!"

"Stop that wailing and beat on those mules when I tighten the slack in the rope. And damn it, cuss! Never mind callin' Moses. Only those long-eared desert canaries can lead you out of the wilderness. Get ready. All right. Lambaste 'em!"

Her saddle rope snapped halfway between the wagon tongue and saddle horn. The mules pulled, but not together. They seesawed, then settled back resignedly in the mud and water that was belly deep around them. And the laden spring wagon seemed to settle a little.

Galt, grinning, happier than he had been in what seemed years, rode down the brush-spotted slope. They did not see him until he was within twenty or thirty feet. And even then did not recognize him on account of his whiskers and the dust that powdered his face and clothes. Aunt Cloe leaned backwards, twisting her bulk out of sight beneath the covered wagon top. To reappear with a shotgun. Then she recognized Galt with a loud wail of thanksgiving.

"Praise de Lawd! Mah prayers is done ansehed!"

Nancy gave a small cry of astonishment and gladness, and her arms went out in a half gesture of welcome that stopped suddenly as the light in her eyes turned cold.

"We didn't holler for your help," she said stiffly.

"Mebby not. But you'd better let me lend a hand before your outfit drops out of sight. You hit the crossing too low. That's quicksand you're bogged in."

And without further argument Galt rode into the mud and water and fastened his catch-rope to the end of the spring-wagon tongue. He handed the end of the rope to Nancy on the bank.

"Take your dallies and make that geldin' of yours pull steady without bustin' my rope. It's the only rope I got. I'll persuade your cold-shouldered, overgrowed pack-rats to do somethin' besides lay down and rest."

Riding alongside the team, he leaned from the saddle and took the lines from Aunt Cloe. He grinned at her and her shining black face beamed. The lines in one hand, he unlooped his quirt from the saddle horn. He stung the rumps of the two wicked-looking little Spanish mules until they woke up to the fact that no unskilled woman was handling them.

The lines in his left hand, he laid the quirt across their mouse-colored hides. And without the aid of the saddle rope Nancy handled, made the mules pull the light spring wagon, with its miscellaneous load of boxes and tin-covered trunks, to solid ground. Though he was splattered with mud and water from head to foot. He handed the lines back to Aunt Cloe who was speechless with admiration. Then he rescued his wet and mud-soiled rope, coiling it slowly as he sat with his weight in one stirrup. Nancy's face was flushed, her eyes bright with humiliation and wrath. Galt eyed her with a faintly humorous grin, though his heart was pounding like a hammer against his ribs.

"I hope," he said carelessly, "that you know where you're goin'."

"I most certainly do," snapped Nancy.

"Because," he went on, as if she had not spoken, "this is a long ways off the main trail. And we've sighted war parties of Kiowas and Comanches since we've been in this part of the country. This crossin' ain't used except by Injuns and some rustlers."

"Rustlers? That accounts, then, for your knowing it so well."

"Injuns!" groaned Aunt Cloe. "Oh, Lawdy, Mistah Galt, git us outa heah. Don' leave us. Honey chile, hush yo' tongue."

"You called me a rustler before," said Galt, his grin fading, "you're 'titled to your own opinion."

"You ran off my cattle. You have my remuda —"

"And shot your father from the brush," Galt cut in. "That's what Lon Coulter told you and that's what you want to believe. You're so stuck on Lon and his ways, I'll take you to him. He's camped not far from here. I reckon it was his camp you're headed for."

"Yes. And I'm not lost. And your Injun talk don't fool anybody but Aunt Cloe. And I'm going to marry Lon Coulter. And I don't thank you for horning in where you weren't wanted and playing the hero. The mules would have pulled out without the beating you gave them. And if that was quicksand instead of just plain old river mud, the wagon and mules would have been pulled under long before you got here. A good way to dry out your rope is to drag it behind you when you head back for your rustler camp. Come on, Aunt Cloe. Let's get going. And we don't need a wagon pilot." She flicked the mules with the end of her broken saddle rope. And as they jumped and started jerkily, Aunt Cloe could do nothing but set up a dismal wail as she tried to keep the wicked-tempered mules on the trail.

"Go back to your rustlers and the queen of the outlaws. Go back to your beloved Rose of Tascosa. Come near me again and I'll take a quirt to you."

Nancy's voice had become an angry shout. She whirled her horse and rode off, her head held tilted at a defiant angle. Though tears were stinging her eyes.

A few moments and she was lost to sight. Aunt Cloe, moaning and wailing, followed. Galt sat his horse, a blank look on his face. What had she meant by mentioning the Rose of Tascosa? Somehow, he reckoned, she must have learned that the Rose of Tascosa was his mother. And therefore he was doubly condemned in Nancy's eyes. The Rose of Tascosa trailed with rustlers. Galt was her son. Therefore, he was a rustler. And every bit of evidence showed to prove it. Perhaps such damning lies as Windy had told had reached her ears. Lon Coulter would see to that. Lon would have told Nancy that the Rose of Tascosa was no better than the dance-hall Magdalenes of Dodge. And Galt was her son. Nancy was as proud as a thoroughbred. And as high strung and touchy. She'd want nothing to do with the son of the Rose of Tascosa.

No wonder she had so resented him. And if Lon had told her, back at Dodge, that Galt was the son of the outlaw queen, then that would account for her actions that night at the graveyard. The Rose of Tascosa had been there that night. Nancy, of course, had seen her. And Lon, wise to the relationship of mother and son, had played his ace in the hole. That accounted for everything.

But Nancy wasn't big enough to give Galt a chance to defend himself. That's what hurt. She was condemning him on the word of Lon Coulter. Just now she had said that she was going to marry Lon. And she was on her way to join him.

It made Galt sick with anger and bitterness. And a white, cold rage gripped him. Nancy wanted to join Lon Coulter. Then he'd see to it that she did. He'd spotted what he reckoned was Lon's camp, yesterday. But Nancy would miss it if she kept on the trail she was taking. Galt swung his horse around and rode across country at a long trot. And about an hour later, still seething with cold anger, he spotted two riders driving a little bunch of cattle. He watched them until he was certain that one of them was Lon Coulter.

Then, figuring the direction they were

taking, sizing up the topography of the country, he swung in a long half-circle and, half an hour later, was squatting in a sheltered ambush of brush and rocks, his gun in his hand.

XIII

"Reach for the sky, Coulter!" Galt barked. "Make a gunplay and I'll kill you and the skunk with you. You don't know what a hell of a lot of pleasure I'd get out of gut-shootin' you."

Galt had Lon and the other man at a distinct disadvantage. They raised their hands slowly. Galt's voice rasped harshly.

"Nancy Curtis, your intended bride, is headed for your camp. But she's on the wrong trail. I'm takin' you to her. But I'm not lettin' this other snake with you ride away from here to give the news out that I'm in the vicinity. So he goes along. And to keep you two rattlers from strikin', I'm drawin' your fangs. Unbuckle your gun belts with your left hands so that your guns drop on the ground. Then drop your saddle guns on the ground, likewise."

"It's a trap to kill us," snarled Lon Coulter.

"If I wanted to kill you, I could do it easy from here, right now. I'm takin' you to the girl you fooled with your dirty lies. And when I'm done workin' you over, you're goin' to tell her the truth about her father. The rest about my mother, the Rose of Tascosa, is up to her to decide about. Shed your guns, snakes. And we'll be on our way. Act purty, now, or I'll kill you both like I'd tromp the heads off two rattlers."

The man with Lon obeyed. Lon reluctantly followed suit. Galt rode from behind his ambush, a twisted grin on his mouth, his eyes hard, cold, bloodshot slits. His six-shooter covered them.

"Head for the trail that leads to the muddy crossin' on the North Fork. Hit a trot. Break into a lope and I'll start shootin'. I'll be ridin' close behind and my gun is in my hand. Git goin'."

Galt herded them ahead of him, watching them closely. One or both of them might have a second six-shooter concealed on his person and might make a desperate play.

Lon Coulter still suspected a trap. He did not for a minute believe that Nancy Curtis was on this part of the open range. He had left her at Dodge at the hotel there and her farewell had been frigid and tinged with suspicion and loathing. She had told him to deliver the trail herd to Dodge and if he lost any of the remuda or the cattle, she'd hold him responsible. Bat Masterson had been present at the time and had told Lon that he had appointed himself Nancy's guardian and, acting as such, suggested that Lon take her orders.

Lon wondered if Galt was drunk or loco or was just leading up to a killing. He had a small derringer pistol in his pants pocket but this was not the time to use it. Galt had him covered, to start with. And he needed a very close range to use the short-barreled little pocket pistol. He'd have to bide his time, watch his chance, and use it at close quarters. Meanwhile, assume an attitude of fear and sullen submission. Not exactly a difficult role, under circumstances.

The man with him was one of the Two Pole Pumpkin reps Galt had sent back to him. The man was growling threats. Galt finally shut him up with a barked command.

Galt herded them along the trail. Had he been less intent on watching his prisoners, he might have sighted a rider who topped a ridge, watched them for some minutes, then rode off in another direction.

Lon Coulter was surprised when they

sighted Nancy Curtis riding ahead of the mule team driven by Aunt Cloe. And he realized that Galt meant to somehow get a confession of the truth concerning Jeff Curtis's death from him. His handsome face went a little white and his jaw muscles knotted tightly. To confess any part of the truth concerning the killing of Jeff Curtis meant death. His only bet was to kill Galt when the chance came. Till then, to keep on with his accusations against Galt. What was that Galt had said about the Rose of Tascosa being his mother? That was an altogether new angle. Had Galt meant it for the truth? Was she really his mother? He'd damn soon find out. Before they reached the place where Nancy and the canvas-topped wagon had halted, he shot a cleverly worded question.

"You and that outlaw mother of yours play a smart game, don't you, Mister Gospel Galt? Kept it mighty secret about her bein' your mother."

"I didn't know she was my mother till a few days ago. And if you want to live long, keep her name off your lyin' tongue."

Lon Coulter smiled thinly as he rode on. He had a new weapon in his hands now. He was almost in a triumphant frame of mind as they rode up to where Nancy, alongside the wagon, sat her horse. Her face was a little white and she had a gun in her hand. Aunt Cloe's eyes were so wide open that the whites rolled like China marbles. Her huge black hands gripped the shotgun.

"I fetched your lover back to you," said Galt coldly. "He's goin' to tell you a few things that I reckon you should know before you're married to him. Put up your gun. Aunt Cloe, will you take a rope and tie this other man's hands and feet so tight that he can't wiggle? If he makes a fuss, knock him in the head with a rock, then tie him. He's one of the men that helped kill Jeff Curtis."

"Sho' enough, Mistah Galt?" Aunt Cloe's hands gripped the shotgun tighter and pointed it towards the man.

"Pecos Moss done the killin'," blurted the man, badly scared and eager to talk himself into Galt's good graces. "Lon knows a-plenty. Don't let that nigger kill me, Gospel! Don't let 'em kill me, Miss Curtis! I never had a thing to do with killin' Jeff Curtis. So help me Gawamighty! Make Lon Coulter tell what —"

"Shut up, you yellow-bellied coyote," snapped Lon, white-lipped. "If you weren't drunk and scared to death, you'd face the music like a man instead of blubbering out lies. Nancy, I brought men to Dodge to prove that Hipshot and Galt Magrath killed poor Uncle Jeff. Hipshot and Galt Magrath had help. The Rose of Tascosa."

"I told you," said Galt, "that I'd kill you if you dirtied her name with your lyin' tongue. And I will, after I've choked some truth out of you with my hands. Aunt Cloe, tie up that other snake. Hurry up. I'm rearin' to get at Lon Coulter."

Aunt Cloe could move fast, for all her bulk. And her manner of trussing up the cursing, begging Pumpkin man was both efficient and rough. Her huge palm cuffed him into silence.

"Ah done fix 'im, Mistah Galt," she puffed, eyeballs rolling. "Ah done tole mah Honey lamb dis heah no account po' white trash Lon Coultah has de tongue of de vipah."

Then Galt played a trump. He took the buckskin-covered Bible from his saddle pocket and handed it to the giant Negress.

"Will you take care of this for me, Aunt Cloe?"

"Yes, *suh*, Ah will. Yes, *suh*, Mistah Gospel Galt. Bet Ah will! As da good Book say, smite 'eh hahd and in de weak places. De Bible an' de sow'd ma'ch side by side into battle. Smite 'at white trash. Fo' de glory ob de Lawd."

"Step down, Coulter," said Galt, unbuckling his gun belt and hanging it over his saddle horn. "I've waited too long for this." He turned towards Nancy who sat her horse in white-lipped silence.

"You might not exactly like this, but you're goin' to watch it, regardless."

Galt stepped off his horse, kicking off his chaps. While Lon did likewise.

A faint smile played around the corners of Lon's tight-lipped mouth. He was Galt's equal in size and weight and he had won more than a few rough-and-tumble fights. Given a little luck and he wouldn't need to use that deadly little derringer pistol hid in his pants pocket. He smiled up at Nancy, then faced Galt.

"Come and get it, you Bible-spoutin' son of a she-rustler. They tell me that the Rose of Tascosa has thorns. Just the same, she's been picked by —"

Galt rushed him with the fury of a cougar. But Lon had been watching for that. He had purposely infuriated his enemy. His fist crashed full into Galt's mouth and nose. Blood spurted. Lon's other fist struck him low in the groin as he staggered off balance.

Then Galt, sick with sudden pain, clinched. They went to the ground with a crash.

Lon Coulter was a past master at dirty fighting. And Galt was taking more punishment than he had ever taken in a fight. For his few fights had been at school where they practiced sportsmanship, or at camp where the rules were mostly fair and few men resorted to gouging and biting and kneeing in the clinches. That low blow had made him sick but he kept Lon tangled in the clinch until he recovered a little. Then he broke loose and scrambled to his feet. And though Lon's teeth had drawn blood from his arm and one eye had been gouged until it was stabbing his brain with dull pain, he kept his head. And did not rush again blindly.

Aunt Cloe was shuffling around, wailing and shouting and praying, waving the old Bible and shouting to the Lord to smite the sinner, while Nancy, white as chalk, gripped the horn of the saddle with one hand, unconsciously still hanging onto her six-shooter with the other hand.

She was speechless with terror, sick a little at the blood and brutality of it. Galt was covered with blood that spurted from his nose and mouth. He looked much worse hurt than he was.

There was no display of boxing science. They slugged and ducked and circled one another. Smashing in hard blows when an opening showed. Now and then feinting, warding off a blow with forearm or shoulder. Going down together in clinches that rolled them in the dust.

Galt, who never smoked to amount to anything, and whose drinking was even less than his smoking, had the better wind. And quick to take advantage of it. He avoided Lon's rushes, feinted him into swinging wildly, and kept him on the move. Until Lon was badly winded and his legs were weakening. And when an opening showed, he stabbed Lon's face with hard lefts that had the latter's face bloody and battered. And when Lon's footwork was no more than clumsy staggering, and his swings lacked power, Galt began to punish him. He knocked Lon down several times. Each time he gave Lon a chance to get back on his feet. Not once did he kick him. If Lon did not get up, he jerked him up and gave him a chance to square off.

Lon's breath was coming in panting, lung-bursting sobs. His clothes were torn, covered with blood and dirt. Though Galt looked little the better for the roughing they had both taken. Galt sent Lon down with a crashing left and right. Lon lay there in the dirt, one arm across his face, the other hidden under him.

"I'm licked," he sobbed chokingly. "Let me alone. I've got all I can take."

"Then tell Nancy who killed her father. Talk, Coulter, or I'll kick the truth out of you. Who killed Jeff Curtis?"

"Let a man . . . get his wind . . . I'll talk. . . ."

Galt stepped back, wiping blood and dirt from his face with his arm. He grinned up at Nancy through the bloody smear.

Then from where Lon lay on the ground came the flash and roar of the wicked little derringer. The twin-barreled little close-range gun belched flame.

Galt was jerked sideways by the force of the two heavy lead slugs that tore across his chest and shoulder. And as he reeled Lon Coulter staggered to his feet. To go down in a heap as Nancy jumped her horse into him. One shod hoof struck Lon a glancing blow on his head and he crumpled and lay in a motionless heap. Then Nancy was off her horse and running towards Galt who stood on widespread legs, his right hand clutching his wounded left chest and shoulder.

"He's killed you, Galt! The murderer! Galt!" Her two hands were touching his torn shoulder, pressing against the wounds that gushed blood. His blood was staining her hands and clothes.

"He just grazed me, that's all. You're gettin' blood all over you."

"What do I care? Aunt Cloe! Do something!"

Aunt Cloe did something. Dead men might scare her out of her wits but she had dressed wounds in her time. Razor cuts when black boys fought for her favors. Knife stabs and gunshot holes in black hides. In a very short time she had Galt's wounds tightly bandaged. She had just finished when Galt saw half a dozen riders topping a distant ridge. They came from the general direction of where he reckoned Lon Coulter's camp was.

"Can you ride a horse?" he asked Aunt Cloe.

"Not since Ah was a chile. Since Ah done growed averdepoise."

Galt looked at her and agreed that she'd never manage it. He looked at the loaded spring wagon. No time to unload its numerous trunks and boxes and camp equipment. He got to his feet. Taking the lines, he cramped the team of mules sharply, and upset the laden covered light wagon with a loud crash that brought a wail from Aunt Cloe.

"Tie some blankets on the running gear of the wagon," he told Aunt Cloe. "We'll come back later for the stuff. You're ridin' the running gears and whipping those mules down the hind leg."

"Don't need no beddin' fo' to cushion mah bones. All Ah takes is 'at Bible an 'at shotgun. An' we sees kin 'em long-eared jackasses fly widout wings."

And Aunt Cloe suited action to her words. Galt managed a grin as he and Nancy mounted.

"Aunt Cloe," he called out as she uncoupled the reach from the front axle, disconnecting the rear wheels and taking her perch on the front axle, settling her bulk solidly and somehow managing the shotgun, stowing the Bible inside her voluminous blouse, and gripping the stock of her whip with its short buckskin lash, "you're ridin' a chariot, shore enough."

"Chariot's good enough fo' angels, it sho' suits 'is heah black sinnah. Whichaway I head 'ese heah gollopin' mules?"

Galt pointed with his gun. "We'll foller behind. You may not look like the pictures I've seen of angels, but you'll do. I'll tell a man, you'll do. Pour the buckskin to 'em, Aunt Cloe. All set, Nancy?"

"All set, Galt. Is Lon — ?"

"Dead? Not this time. He's comin' alive. You saved my life, Honey. If I wasn't such a mess I'd kiss you."

Nancy crowded her horse against his, leaned from the saddle and kissed him. Blood, whiskers, dirt and all. She kissed him. And they rode away in the dust kicked up by Aunt Cloe's little mules that were under the impression that they were running away.

Lon's men delayed where they found him. And their chase was only half-hearted as they took in after Galt and Nancy and Aunt Cloe. And about five miles from the start of the flight, Galt sighted a bunch of his riders.

"We're safe now, Nancy. Those are my cowpunchers. That's luck."

But Galt's gay spirits took a downward plunge as he recognized one of the riders as one of Hipshot's men. He had a blood-stained bandage on one arm and his face was haggard, gray with fatigue and pain. The other cowpunchers all wore that look of men who bring evil tidings.

"Pecos Moss's men jumped us," said the wounded man from Hipshot's outfit. "Three nights ago. Stampeded the herd and shot hell out of us."

"Hipshot?" Galt's voice was a dry, harsh whisper. "Hipshot's killed?"

"He's all right. He sent for men. It's the Rose of Tascosa that got shot. Pecos Moss shot her at Tascosa. She sent for you. She wants to see you before she dies."

The Rose of Tascosa. Galt's mother. The woman whom life had so roughly treated. That strangely hard, beautiful woman who was his mother, and yet a stranger to him. She was dying. She wanted to see her son before she died. Galt nodded dully. He did not see Nancy watching him. She had gone a little white and a hardness had chilled the warmth of her eyes.

"The boys will take you on to camp," Galt told Nancy, and his voice sounded lifeless. "I've got to go."

Nancy had no way of knowing that the Rose of Tascosa was Galt's mother. All she knew of this woman called the Rose of Tascosa was that she was the leader of outlaws. Nancy had seen her but once. The night that Galt had preached at the Dodge graveyard. Nancy had seen a strikingly beautiful face, crowned with a mass of burnished copper-hued hair. And she had heard the Rose of Tascosa's voice, throaty, vibrant, tense, talking to Hipshot.

"Galt is the most precious thing in my life. It's the love of him that's like a knife blade twisted in my heart. Can't you understand? I must have him. I've *got* to have him, Hipshot. I want him with me forever and always. In spite of everything this side of heaven or hell. He loved me once, more than anything in the world. . . . You think he'll love me again, Hipshot?"

Nancy remembered every word she had overheard that night. Every inflection, every shading of that vibrant voice of the woman with the breathtakingly beautiful face and thick coppery hair. And Hipshot had replied:

"You bet he'll love you. He's never quit lovin' you."

"Then get him away from this place, before they kill him. Use my men. I'll cover your getaway. Take him to Tascosa. I'll meet you there. Galt's mine and God or the devil can't keep me from having him. . . ."

Memory of it all came back with a rush now to Nancy. Galt's face, hard lined, stern. His eyes dark with some deep pain. And he repeated in that flat, toneless voice:

"I've got to go."

"Of course." Nancy's stiff lips formed the words.

"You understand."

"I understand perfectly. Don't mind me."

Galt's good arm went around her shoulders as he leaned from the saddle, their stirrups touching. She let his bruised, unshaven lips kiss her roughly. And he did not seem to realize that she had not returned his farewell

238

caress. He let her go and started off. Then reined up.

"Hand me my Bible, Aunt Cloe."

He shoved the Bible in his saddle pocket. Then spurred his horse to a long lope, the wounded man from Hipshot's outfit riding with him. Without a backward glance at Nancy who, the color drained from her face and lips, watched his going through terribly hurt, horribly shocked eyes. Galt could have struck her and the hurt would have been as nothing.

XIV

Galt was astonished to find Bat Masterson at camp. The Marshal of Dodge had fetched a dozen men with him. He was hunting for Nancy Curtis.

"She slipped out of Dodge while I was in Abilene on business."

"She'll be along directly. You'll take her back to Dodge?"

"Even if I have to handcuff her."

Bat Masterson already knew the news about the Rose of Tascosa. And it seemed as though he was one of the very few who knew that she was Galt's mother. He had known it all along. And there was no doubting his high opinion of her.

"As fine a woman as ever lived, Galt. The only cattle she ever rustled, she took away from cattle thieves. The money she got from the proceeds she used to help unfortunate women like herself. They call her an outlaw. But there's many of us who call her an angel of mercy. You'll find her at Tascosa where Frank Curtis took her after she'd been shot. Pecos Moss shot her when he learned that Frank wasn't dead. Seems like Lon Coulter had seen Frank one night in Dodge when he slipped in after dark to have the doctor cut a bullet or two out of his hide. It was the night you preached at the graveyard. Lon told Pecos that Frank was alive. And Pecos ketched on that the Rose had set a trap for him. He trailed her and shot her. Pecos has organized every renegade west of the Pecos and you and Hipshot have a job cut out for yourselves. You look badly shot up, Gospel. Take it easy."

"It's just a flesh wound. No bones busted. Aunt Cloe tied it up as good as a sawbones. Strapped it tight to my side to keep it from busting open and bleeding. Just a scratch."

"I'll take care of Nancy. And we'll hold the herd here till Spud Dulin's men get here. He's takin' charge of the cattle. As Nancy's legal guardian I sold all the cattle that belonged to Jeff Curtis, likewise the remuda, to Spud at his own price which was more than market value. This outfit belongs to him now. He's sent men to help Hipshot. You're workin' now for Spud Dulin. And for yourself. Son, when you whupped that barber they call Sport McAllister, you dealt yourself four aces and the joker."

So it was with mingled emotions milling crazily in his mind that Galt saddled a fresh horse and headed for Tascosa. Riding a south by west course into a sunset streaked blood red.

It was a race against death and Galt spared neither himself nor the horse he rode. But though he pushed his horse to the limit it seemed that they were crawling at a snail's pace. And because he was uncertain as to any chance relay of fresh mounts, he must calculate the distance of about a hundred and fifty miles and gauge his pace accordingly. Galt knew how to get the most out of a horse without killing the animal.

Bat Masterson had wanted to send a man or two with him across that dangerous strip of country, but Galt wanted to go alone.

"One man is less apt to be sighted than three or four. And even if I am sighted, the chances are they won't take the trouble to head me off just to read my brand. The few renegade Injuns on the prowl are after horses or cattle. They ain't botherin' with a lone rider. And the same goes for the rustlers. I stand a good chance of slippin' through without firin' a shot. I'd rather go alone."

So he traveled alone, forking the best horse in the remuda. And as he rode he asked God to let his mother live. Galt wanted to make up to her for the terrible wrong Preacher Sam had done. And it seemed that God should give him a chance to make his mother understand that Preacher Sam had not meant to be so unjust. His ways had been harsh and stern and rock-bound. Preacher Sam had not, for all the countless times he read the Book, ever learned the true, deep meanings of its teachings. Because something in his early youth must have stifled in his heart real pity and tolerance and understanding and love. Preacher Sam's make-up had been barren of softer things like that. In bone and muscle and mind and heart he had been as hard as the very cliffs of the surf-beaten rocky shores of his birthplace in the extreme north of Ireland where he had spent his boyhood days. His father before him had been a hard man who wrested from a barren, unyielding, stubborn bit of land a bare existence. And had been forced to flee his homeland because of political strife. He had been forced from Ireland, from his thatched-roofed, poverty bare home on the northernmost tip of County Donegal, to make his own hard way in America. And had instilled his own bitterness in the heart of his son Sam who had been orphaned in a foreign land. So Preacher Sam had his heritage of hardness and narrowed prejudices and ideas of right and wrong. And it had taken the blood of Mary Galt to soften the Magrath hardness in Galt. And Galt understood that. It was that which he wanted to tell his mother. That, and many other things. Before she died. Before she died hating God and the Book which He had left behind on earth when the man Christ had died on the cross.

Galt Magrath, Gospel Galt, was carrying a bloodstained Bible to his dying mother. And he asked God to let her live until he reached her. And after that to let the Rose of Tascosa get well so that she would know real happiness and the love of her own son. Galt wanted to tell her of the lonely nights of his boyhood when his pillow had been wet with tears and his heart had ached for her. She must live long enough to know how much he had missed her, how empty his boyhood years had been without her. How barren of love his youth had been, after that night when his father had taken him from her at Dodge. And perhaps she would find it in her

244

heart to forgive Preacher Sam Magrath for the terrible wrong he had done.

"Please, God, don't let her die!" Galt kept saying aloud.

And though his lips were clamped and silent, every beat of his pulse must have been repeating that prayer as he rode, just before dawn, through a rocky, brush-filled canyon. And blundered into the danger that was hidden there in the black shadows of the night.

It was the nicker of a horse that jerked Galt awake, his gun in his hand. And then, before his blinking heavy-lidded eyes had focused to the shadows, a rasping challenge:

"*Quien es? Quien es?*"

Galt whirled his horse. But the back trail was blocked by a swarm of men. They were all around him in such numbers that he could not make them out. They were crowded thick on all sides. His horse reared and lunged as men swung on the bridle reins. Hands reached up, pulling him out of the saddle. He came down fighting, clubbing at the tangle of heads and flailing arms with the barrel of his six-shooter. Then something struck him on the head and knocked him unconscious.

He woke to find his legs tied together and his arms tied behind him. And in the light of a small campfire he stared at dark, sinister-looking faces. A motley gang of Mexicans, Indians and 'breeds. A big Mexican with graying hair and mustache glowered at him. He seemed to be the leader. Then he grinned and his dark face looked even more evil than before. He had a skinning knife in his hand and tested its whetted edge on a calloused thumb, grinning the wider, showing powerful yellow teeth.

"We shall start first with the ears," he said in thick English, and Galt caught the odor of fetid breath, rank with bad whiskey.

"The both ears. Then the nose and one by one the fingers and the thombs and after that the toes. I bet you don't like that, eh?"

There was no doubting the intentions of the half-drunken Mexican. He was not bluffing. Though Galt's head was splitting with pain from the blow that had knocked him senseless, he could think clearly enough. He was in the hands of one of the renegade packs that were the scum and dregs of that part of the country. Cowardly unless they were in a pack, then brave only when they outnumbered the enemy many times over. They preyed upon the ranchers and trail herds and wagon trains that were constantly on the move. This pack of human jackals would show a man no mercy. There was enough of the bad blood of mixed races in their veins to delight in the torture of prisoners.

"Which ear you want to lose first, eh, gringo?"

"You have a market for my ears?" questioned Galt in Mexican.

"Market? You mean to sell these ears of yours?"

"That's it. Who'll pay you for the ears or the fingers or toes you're going to cut off my body?"

"Nobody would pay for such rotten meat."

"Just what I thought. Which proves that you are either a born fool or you are too drunk to use your burro brains. If you had gold in your hand would you throw it away? No. If you had a horse worth much money would you cut his ears and legs off? Or would you take the horse to Tascosa and sell him for enough money to buy all the whiskey in town? I don't know who you are, hombre, but I know that you must have the brains of a burro. Otherwise you would put away your knife and make a bargain. With my ears and hands and feet cut off, I am not worth much. But deliver me alive in Tascosa and I can put gold in your pockets and whiskey in your bellies."

"Pah! What good is gold in the pockets of a man hanging to a tree? What good is a belly full of whiskey if there are bullet holes in the belly so that it leaks out faster than you can pour it in from a jug. They would kill any one of us who was loco enough to show his face in Tascosa. I think I cut off first the left ear. . . ."

"Either one," said Galt through set teeth, determined to die as game as possible. "But before you commence whittling, hombre, listen with your dirty ears to what I tell you and these others. If I am not in Tascosa within a certain time, men will hunt for me. They will find me dead here with my body mutilated. And they will track every damned man of you down and kill you. Because you have killed the son of the Rose of Tascosa. You have kept that son of hers from reaching her bedside before she dies. You know the name of the Rose of Tascosa, no? You know then what her men will do to you if you kill her son. That is all, hombre. I have warned you. Go ahead with your damned knife. I will show you how a brave man meets death. You will see that the son of the Rose of Tascosa is not afraid to die while cowards look on."

"The Rose of Tascosa has no son, gringo. You lie!"

Galt had seen the others back away at the mention of her name. He saw their eyes staring at him, and heard some of them whispering. And the mustached leader was beginning to hesitate. Plainly, he was not sure of himself.

"For the Rose of Tascosa," said the Mexican, "any man of us would die fighting. But you lie when you say you, a grown man, are the son of her who is too young and too beautiful to be your mother. You are ugly and have a beard on your skin. Pah! Lies of a coward!" But Galt saw hesitation in his bloodshot, evil eyes.

"If you have the guts of a rabbit you will take me to her then, and prove that I lie. I tell you I am her son. She is dying and sent for me. In my saddle pocket is the Bible I take to read from to her before she dies. Look you in my saddle pockets, burro brains. And move pronto. My time is being wasted. If she dies before I reach her, then the curse of God will be on you. Put me on my horse and take me to her, thou son-of-a-he-goat." And Galt followed up his advantage by roundly cursing the drunken Mexican.

One of the crowd produced the buckskin-covered Bible which he had stolen from the saddle pocket. Another peered into Galt's face, straightened tipsily, and nodded with drunken gravity at the leader.

"He has whiskers on his face, and much dirt and blood and his nose is out of joint and swollen but he is the man I saw once at the house of the Señora where the Rose of Tascosa sometimes stays when she is in town. He came there with the Señor Frank Curtis. And left later with that wicked old *barrachon*, Hipshot. No doubt he lies when he says the young and beautiful Rose of Tascosa is the mother of such a big hulk. But just the same we had better take him there. And leave on the ears on his head. If he is valuable to her, she may reward us."

"That is what I intended to do in the first place," growled the leader. "I was just feeling him out for courage. Saddle the horses. *Pronto.* Cut loose his arms and legs but keep his guns. Put him on a fresh horse. If you are worth gold, gringo, we will soon find out. *Andale!* Let's go!"

It was getting dawn when they started. Galt, with the assistance of one of the gang who was less drunk than the others, bathed and bandaged his wounded shoulder and chest and strapped it tightly to prevent further loss of blood. He drank enough of their whiskey to dull the throbbing pain, and wolfed cold beans and tortillas and jerked meat. The horse he was given was one of the stolen Mill Iron horses and a good one. And though he was a prisoner, they began to treat him with more respect as the miles went by, and nightfall, after a long, hard ride, brought them to the lights of Tascosa.

At the edge of town they halted. And with only the leader and one other man as guards, Galt rode to the lighted adobe at the edge of town where he had parted from his mother a couple or three weeks before. The Mexican woman, who seemed to have no name except the Señora, met them at the door. In the lighted room behind her, Galt caught a glimpse of candles burning in red glass before a small shrine. A crucifix showing in the flickering candle-light. She was in black, with a black shawl covering her head, and in her hands she held a rosary. She was sobbing loudly.

Then Frank Curtis came from a room beyond and moved past the weeping figure in black and went outside. There was a gun in his hand. He shoved it back in its holster when he recognized Galt in the light that came from the open doorway.

"That you, Galt? Thank God you got here. Get down."

"I'm roped to the saddle horn. Is she dying?"

One of the Mexicans cut Galt's hands loose and he got stiffly from the saddle. He swayed a little as he stood beside his horse, hanging to the saddle horn.

"She's going to die?" he asked as Frank took his arm.

"The doctor gives her an even chance to pull through. You're hurt, Galt."

"I'll be all right. Take me to her."

"She's sleepin' now. The doctor give her sleepin' medicine to ease the pain. I'll get you cleaned up. You're a mess, boy. Bloody as a butcher." He led Galt towards the door.

"I told these two drunken cut-throats I'd pay 'em if they fetched me here."

Frank glared at them. Then told the weeping Señora to give them some money and send them away. He took Galt into a bedroom where there was a wash-stand with bucket and basin. And set about cleaning him up.

"Take a big slug of that whiskey while I get you clean clothes and a razor. You want to look decent when you see her. Did you fetch your Bible along?"

"Yes."

"Good. You'll need it. And you'll need more than that to save your mother's life."

"You said the doctor gives her an even chance?"

"Yes. But unless you can save her, she'll die. She'll die because she don't want to live. She don't say so, but I know. She's not going to fight for her life. That's why she is going to die. . . ."

Galt was shaved and had on clean clothes when he went in to see his mother. She smiled at him as he bent over her. She looked more beautiful than ever, her face a creamy white, her glorious hair pillowing her head. As Galt knelt beside the bed, Frank Curtis tip-toed out of the room, leaving them together.

"Forgive me," she whispered against his cheek, "for the way —"

"I understand, mother. More than you know. There isn't anything to forgive. We need each other and I'm never going to leave you. I'm not going to let you die, either. I need you too much to let you go. All these years I've needed you. Hipshot and I hunted all over for you. Now I've found you and it wouldn't be fair to either of us if you let yourself die. Please fight, mother. . . ."

"Talk to me, Galt. Tell me all about yourself. Tell me about this little Nancy girl you're in love with. Now don't tell me you're not in love with her. Frank told me all about her. She must be splendid. She'd better be. And what's all this about Spud Dulin putting his PD brand on you? And tell me about shoving Sport McAllister in the rain barrel. And how did you get this black eye and swollen nose and what's the matter with your shoulder? You know I can't die in peace till I get all those questions answered. And a lot more. You don't know how proud I am to be the mother of such a fighting sky-pilot. When you win over gun toters like Doc Holliday and those other gambling gents at Dodge, you have to be better than just ordinary. Doc cleaned Sport McAllister down to his pet razor when you showed up to preach at poor little Virginia's funeral. And the dance-hall girls at Dodge City want to build you a church. And Mysterious Dave promises to furnish the congregation and pass the hat. And Hipshot told me how you saved Lon Coulter's life after that dude was going to hang you. Bat Masterson says you're all right. You've gone a long ways, Galt. I'm proud of you. And even with that black eye and that Roman nose you're mighty handsome." She held his head in her two hands and laughed up at him.

"Then you won't die? You'll put up a fight? You won't leave me, now that we've found each other?"

"They've called me everything but a quitter, son. Not even my worst enemies call me that." She pulled his face down to hers and kissed him. Then she made Galt pull up a chair and talk to her while she held tightly to his hand, sometimes rubbing her cheek against it while she plied him with questions. And when he had finished talking, she looked at him, her smile softening her face, her eyes dark, no longer hard.

"You haven't asked me a single question," she said.

"No. There's nothing to ask."

"You've heard me called a bad woman, Galt. But I'm not bad in the way they mean. Let me put my hand on Preacher Sam Magrath's Bible and swear it. I want to."

At her insistence, Galt brought out the Bible. And the Rose of Tascosa put her slim, white hand on it. In measured, low-toned words she swore her solemn oath.

"Because," she said, smiling at him, "you'll want to marry Nancy Curtis. And she's entitled to the truth. You can tell her that your mother was not a wanton. Now kiss me, Galt. Then send Frank in. There are some things I want to tell him."

Galt held her closely in his arms and she clung to him almost desperately. Then she let him go and lay back on her pillow, her eyes closed, a smile on her pale face.

Galt found Frank Curtis outside. "She's

not going to die, Frank. She's happy. She wants to see you."

Galt sat down on a bench outside. Inside the candle-lit room that joined the bedroom where the Rose of Tascosa lay, the black-clad Señora knelt before the shrine with its crude, hand-carved and painted wooden image of Christ on the Cross. Telling her rosary beads in a chant that was muted.

Galt was alone under the stars. Alone with his dreams. Smiling to himself as he remembered his mother's great happiness. So that he did not know just when Frank Curtis joined him. They sat together in silence for a while. Then Frank Curtis spoke.

"Your mother is dead, Galt."

XV

"She wanted it that way," Frank Curtis explained to Galt as they rode away from her grave at sunrise.

"She knew best, son. It was just after she had kissed you good-by that she managed to slip the bandage off the wound in her side. She bled to death slowly. Her end was happy. She did not want you to see her go. And she wanted you to read from the Bible when we laid her to rest. That was her way of telling you all the things she could not put into words. She knowed you'd understand."

Galt nodded. He understood, now. They rode on in silence. Then Frank Curtis spoke again.

"She never married me. And Hipshot told you the reason why she would not. She believed that I killed Preacher Sam. And because she was not going to do anything to hurt you, her son, she would not marry the man who had killed your father."

"Then you did kill him?" Somehow Galt could not rouse himself to anger against this man.

"I meant to. . . . So help me God, I don't know whether or not I killed Sam Magrath. I don't know. . . . I was coming up the trail with the San Saba Pool herd. I was going to kill Sam Magrath when I cut his sign. But I wasn't going to bushwhack him. I sent him a fair warning. I told him to get a gun and be ready to use it when he met me. And I told him why I was going to kill him. Because he had treated your mother the way he had. I told him to keep his friend Hipshot with him. And I sent the same warning to Hipshot. That I was going to kill Preacher Sam Magrath where I found him and that I'd take the two of them on at the same time. Because I figured that Hipshot had some sort of hand in the way your mother got treated. Though I know now I was dead wrong about Hipshot.

"As I calculated, Preacher Sam showed up at the San Saba Pool one night. I called him aside and asked him if he had a gun. He said no. I made him take an extra six-shooter I had. It was just between him and me, understand, and there was no need to let Pecos Moss or any other of the San Saba Pool outfit in on it. So we talked private. I told him to saddle his mule and ride out about five miles, when second guard went on. I was standing second guard that night.

"Because I knew he wasn't used to guns, and when he said Hipshot wasn't in that part of the country within call to stand by him, I told Preacher Sam to pick some place along the trail that crossed the Staked Plains and lay for me. That would give him the advantage and a bushwhacker's shot if he wanted it. And I figured any man would take it under the circumstances. He agreed.

"I went on second guard. As we'd agreed, I quit the herd and headed along the trail. When I'd gone a few miles and no sign of Preacher Sam, I got the notion he'd turned rabbit on me and hit the trail and was whippin' down the hind leg for safer parts.

"Then a shot came from a patch of brush. It knocked me off my horse. I shot at the flash of the gun. And the next shot hit me and that's all I remember.

"So help me God, Galt, that's the truth. It was two weeks later that I regained consciousness. I was in the adobe house at Tascosa, the house where she died last night.

"She was there with me. She nursed me

back to life. And when I was strong enough, she told me that she'd found me out there on the Staked Plains when she was riding alone. At first she thought I was dead. Because I was shot twice and in bad shape. And not twenty feet from where I laid, was the dead body of Preacher Sam Magrath.

"Because I was alive and Preacher Sam was dead, because we'd been pardners since the day I found her at Dodge City in the hotel after she'd tried to kill herself, she let Preacher Sam's dead body lay there. And she loaded me on my horse and somehow got me plumb to Tascosa. I had some life in my shot-up carcass and she was fightin' to save it. To dig a grave with no tools but her hands would have taken time. And time meant a lot just then if she hoped to save me. So don't blame her for not buryin' Preacher Sam."

"I don't. You say she tried to kill herself at Dodge?"

"The night Preacher Sam left town with you and left her alone there in the hotel without a friend to turn to in the toughest town along the cattle trail. The bullet glanced off her ribs. She must have been shakin' bad, and half out of her mind. I taken her to the Señora's. She had a house at the edge of Dodge where she entertained

Mexican cowhands. The Señora and I nursed her back to where she wanted to live. And from then on she rode with me a lot. We camped together and shared the good and the bad. Pardners, Galt, and nothin' more. Though we was as much in love as a man and woman could be. And her hatin' all men and God to boot.

"I wanted to kill Preacher Sam then but she swore she'd quit me if I did. Made me swear I'd never kill him and that I'd never even meet him unless by plumb accident. She told me that some day she was goin' to punish Preacher Sam more than he'd hurt her. She was goin' to wait till you was old enough to make a hand. Then she was goin' to find you and make an outlaw of you. . . . Don't be too hard on her, Galt. His treatment of her had done something to her heart and her mind. And she hated you because you were his flesh and blood and even when you was small, you was the image of your father.

"Then I couldn't stand it any longer. I loved her. And couldn't marry her while Sam Magrath was alive. So I made up my mind to kill him. And without her knowin' it, I sent word to Preacher Sam and to Hipshot.

"And then she found him dead and me

shot to hell with my gun in my hand, an empty shell under the hammer. She asked me if I'd killed Preacher Sam. I hadn't any answer. I still haven't. There's the story, Galt. And I've only one favor to ask before you turn against me. Pecos Moss killed my Rose of Tascosa. I'm trailin' him down. Will your grudge against me wait till I do that job?"

"It'll wait longer than that, Frank," said Galt. "There's no grudge to settle between you and me. You're forgettin' some things. You were the best friend my mother had. She loved you. You saved my life. And anyhow we've been friends right from the time we met."

Frank Curtis gripped the hand Galt held out. Then Galt spoke, breaking a silence.

"Did you tell Hipshot what you've told me?"

"No. He hasn't given me a chance. And even then he wouldn't believe me. He knows I was with the San Saba Pool when Preacher Sam was killed. The sign around where he found Preacher Sam's body was plenty plain. When Rose — I named your mother the Rose of Tascosa; gave her a new name to go with her new life — when Rose patched up the bullet holes in my chest and head, she cut off the coat and shirt I was wearing and left 'em there. Likewise my hat that wouldn't fit on my bandaged head. The hat and coat had my name in 'em. Hipshot found 'em there. No wonder he thinks I killed Preacher Sam. You can't blame him for hatin' me. He thought a heap of Preacher Sam, for some reason."

"Then Hipshot, even when he fetched me the news of my father's death, suspected you. And I reckon I know why he didn't tell me. He was afraid I'd get killed. I've heard him say you were faster than most gun slingers that bragged about the notches on their guns."

Frank Curtis nodded. "But that wasn't all that was on Hipshot's mind. When he gave you your father's Bible, did he give you anything else? Was there anything in the Bible I mean, that belonged to your mother?"

"No. Why, no. What do you mean?"

More than once Frank Curtis, during the short time he and Galt had been together, had hinted such a question, putting it to Galt in various disguised ways.

"I reckon Hipshot didn't tell you much, then. Your mother's wedding ring, with her initials and your father's engraved on the inside, was in the Bible that Hipshot found alongside the dead body of Preacher Sam. Your mother put it there when she examined him and made sure he was dead. A woman would know why she did it, I reckon. Though it was certainly a dead giveaway that she had bin there."

"Hipshot said one night in Dodge," said Galt slowly, "that he had suspicions that he didn't dare tell me. I knew that he was badly worked up about you and the Rose of Tascosa. It was when I told him I'd sighted a woman in town with Pecos Moss."

"That was when we were settin' the trap for Pecos and Lon to make a deal for the cattle that belonged to my brother Jeff. Pecos and Lon figured me dead then. I found out later that Lon spotted me when I went to the doctor's to have him cut a couple of slugs out that Pecos Moss's bush-whackers had put in my hide."

"Hipshot thought a heap of my mother, Frank. He must have suffered the torments of hell thinkin' she had a part in my father's killin'. He liked them both. And he tried to keep me from thinkin' bad towards her. He's the best friend a boy ever had."

"Amen to that. Hipshot didn't want to be-lieve anything bad about Rose. But there was her wedding ring in Preacher Sam's Bible. And it was her that told Hipshot that he'd find Preacher Sam's dead body at a cer-tain place of the Staked Plains. She found him drunk in town and told him. Then slipped away so he couldn't trail her and locate me to kill me.

"When he met her at the graveyard that night at Dodge, he asked her point-blank if she'd had a part in the killing of Preacher Sam, she said no. He made her swear it by the love she bore her son that was standin' with his dead father's Bible in his hand, there by an open grave. And she took an oath that she was innocent. And Hipshot, being wise as a tree full of owls, guessed that the reason she never married me was because she was sure I'd killed your father. And that's why Hipshot reckons it is up to him to square the debt of Preacher Sam Magrath. And he's plumb right."

"You mean that —"

"That now the Rose of Tascosa is dead. And there's nothing to stand in his way. That was the agreement between Hipshot and me."

"You can't do this to me, Frank! You and Hipshot are the best friends I have on earth! It's not fair to yourselves or to my mother or to Preacher Sam or to me. Give me your word not to shoot it out with Hipshot till the three of us have a medicine talk. You didn't kill my father."

"You believe that, Galt?"

"If you'd killed him, I'd know, somehow. That sounds childish as hell but I'd stake my life on it."

"Even the Rose of Tascosa couldn't have the belief you have in me, Galt. My own brother Jeff figured I'd killed Preacher Sam. And, like Hipshot, he figgered I was in with Pecos Moss on the San Saba Pool deal. Hipshot, right now, thinks that. Pecos Moss and Lon Coulter used it as a bait to lead Jeff into the trap at Las Vegas. Lon faked a note signed with my name askin' Jeff to meet me at Las Vegas. Pecos ribbed Lon into writin' the note. Lon's weak, thataway. And treacherous as a snake. And a born forger. Handy with a pen as he is with a runnin' iron."

"Which reminds me," said Galt, and from the tally book he carried, be took the two notes that had come into his hands at Dodge. One left at Bat Masterson's office or home, the other shoved under Nancy's door at the hotel. The notes accusing Galt and Hipshot of the murder of Jeff.

"Lon wrote these. He either delivered 'em himself or had one of his men do it. Or mebby Pecos."

"Frank, what do you aim to do when you cut the sign of Pecos Moss and Lon Coulter?"

"I'll kill Pecos Moss on sight. It'll be

266

harder to kill Lon. He's kinfolks and he'll be scared of me."

"Did it ever occur to you that it might be Pecos Moss that killed Preacher Sam Magrath?" asked Galt.

"It has. Many a time. But he'd never admit it. I'm plumb certain that Rose had some scheme in mind to get him to brag about killin' Preacher Sam to git on the right side of her. But when he found out she hated him like he'd hate a snake, he shot her."

"Pecos Moss hates me," said Galt. "He probably killed my father. He killed my mother. You got to admit, Frank, that killin' Pecos Moss is my job. I've got prior rights, as the law says in fancy words. And before I kill Pecos Moss he's goin' to confess to the murder of my father."

"Pecos Moss, son, is faster with a gun than any man I ever saw in action. Drunk or sober, he's chain lightnin'. You wouldn't have the ghost of a chance."

"That's what they told a gent named David. But he won his scrap with a big cuss called Goliath." Galt grinned faintly, but his eyes were hard as chilled steel. . . .

XVI

There is that old saying about fools tromping heavy-like where angels dare not tip-toe. Nobody ever called Spud Dulin a fool and neither Frank Curtis or Hipshot would have recognized an angel if they'd met one. But when Spud Dulin literally and figuratively stepped between the two enemies he did a job that even a bullet-proof angel wouldn't have been ashamed to brag about afterwards.

It happened at the round-up when Galt and Frank Curtis, fresh from Tascosa and the grave of the Rose of Tascosa, rode up at dusk.

"Before you two bulls lock horns," growled the big cattleman, his beard jutting belligerently, "I'm hornin' in and pawin' some dust in your eyes and bellerin' louder than the both of you. This bein' my range, it's my dirt I'm pawin'.

"I got reason to know that you two gents is both on the prod. And I don't give a damn much what it's all about. But you're bein' ornery and plumb selfish about the feud, whatever it is. You've both helped gather what cattle is in the herd we're holdin' here. And you're both workin' now for old Spud Dulin. And when men work for me they take my orders and listen with both ears to my bellerin'. Pecos Moss and his renegades is somewhere right now drivin' the taller off a big bunch of the cattle I bought from little Nancy Curtis. I'm aimin' to overtake that gent and git back them dogies. They've bin run so much now that they ain't worth a damn except to enter in a race. But they're mine from the tips of their long horns to the end of their bushy tails, and I'm goin' to take 'em. And I'm goin' to hang the hides of Pecos Moss and his rustlers on the fence. But I can't do it without you two gents. You both savvy Pecos and how he works. Like I was tellin' ol' Hipshot, it takes a rustler to ketch a rustler. And that's why I'm payin' you two gents ten times what any man is worth to git Pecos Moss. Pecos Moss and Lon Coulter, to be more exact. I want 'em both. But I want 'em alive. I want them two curly wolves delivered on the hoof to Bat Masterson at Dodge City. For special reasons of my own. I'm offerin' five thousand dollars apiece for Pecos Moss and Lon Coulter. But alive, understand? They ain't worth a plugged dime to me dead.

"Hipshot, you and Frank Curtis has got to bury the hatchet till we gather in them two hombres. Even if the reward money sounds like chicken feed to two empty-pocketed rustlers like yourselves, there's another reason why you two gun-totin' fools have to keep your quarrel on ice for a spell. That reason is settin' his horse yonder. The boy on that played-out sorrel. Meanin' none other than young Gospel. Hell, can't you two boneheads see that the boy is eatin' his heart out with worry? He thinks, for some damn-fool unknown mysterious reason, that you two thick-skulled cow servants are his pardners and that you're both a couple of aces in a new deck. Of course he's wronger than hell but that won't keep him from grievin' deep in his heart because the two best friends he has in the world shoot the bellies off one another with him lookin' on. Now do you two idiots bury the hatchet and smoke the peace pipe or will I take a active hand in this little argument and make it a three-cornered game? Hipshot, shake hands with Frank Curtis."

"I won't shake hands," said Hipshot, "but I'm willin' to let all bets ride till we gather in Pecos Moss and Lon Coulter. Because I got a hankerin' to make them two snakes crawl on their bellies to Bat Masterson and Nancy Curtis and clear me and Galt of the charge of murderin' Jeff."

"That's hoss sense, Hipshot. How about you, Frank?"

Frank Curtis nodded and grinned faintly at Galt, who heaved a sigh of relief. Then Frank looked straight at Hipshot.

"The Rose of Tascosa died last night. Galt will tell you." He reined his horse and rode over to the rope corral to unsaddle.

Spud Dulin rode alongside Galt and put his big hand on Galt's good shoulder.

"Your mother was a mighty fine woman, son. I'm sorry."

Hipshot and Galt walked off a ways together after Galt had turned his leg-weary horse loose and caught a night horse from the remuda inside the rope corral.

"We had a long talk before she died," Galt told Hipshot. "She died happy. She didn't want to live."

"I reckon I understand, son."

"I know about the wedding ring you found in the Bible, Hipshot. Frank didn't kill my father."

"You heard what I told Spud Dulin," said Hipshot flatly.

And Galt knew that tone of voice too well to pursue the subject of Frank Curtis's innocence. After all, what was there he could say that would convince Hipshot, who was strong willed beyond the point of stubbornness. Hipshot would only grin bleakly at Galt's belief in Frank's innocence. Galt remembered that even the Rose of Tascosa had died half believing that the man she loved had killed Preacher Sam Magrath.

Galt took another tack. "After all, Hipshot, Preacher Sam was my father. It's up to me to decide about Frank."

"I knowed Preacher Sam Magrath before you was born," said Hipshot gruffly. And changed the subject.

"Let's fix that shoulder of yourn. And git you a stiff drink. You're as peaked lookin' as a wind-bellied calf. That is, if Spud Dulin ain't emptied the keg. He showed up here with the story about you whuppin' hell out of Lon Coulter and him takin' a pot shot at you with a gambler's peashooter and Nancy tromped her pony on him. Then you hightailed it, leavin' her a-thinkin' you was goin' to meet your outlaw sweetheart. Yeah. Seems like there was a bug that was eatin' on Nancy that night at Dodge and from then on till Bat Masterson and Spud told her different at the camp, after you'd lit out for Tascosa when you got word your mother was dyin'. No wonder she spoke right out loud at the funeral. Wimmen has a jealous streak in 'em wider than the range Spud Dulin claims. Which is some wide. Nancy wanted to light out for Tascosa to ketch you, and Bat had to all but set her afoot till she calmed down. Even so she wouldn't go back to Dodge the next day. She went to Tascosa. Bat went with her. She went there to nurse your mother. To be with her. . . . Ol' Spud was so worked up about it all that he like to drunk the keg dry. Though even if you was to kill off all the rustlers on earth and become President of the States and King of Turkey to boot, he'd still claim that them accomplishments and great deeds was nothin' compared to duckin' Sport McAllister in the water barrel. There he is, waitin' at the keg. Come on while there's a cupful left. . . ."

A killer of the breed to which Pecos Moss belonged, will brag of his gun notches. But no torture, no threat of death will ever drag from him the admission that he killed a defenseless sky-pilot like Preacher Sam. Galt and Hipshot knew that Preacher Sam had been shot in the back. Galt knew because

Hipshot had told him so. And Hipshot hadn't lied. The old range tramp, who could read signs like an Indian, and had closely examined the single gunshot wound that had killed the circuit-rider preacher, had seen more than had the Rose of Tascosa. The sign had told Hipshot that Preacher Sam had been shot in the back as he rode along on his mule. He had been shot from the brush patch. It had been murder.

Here was Hipshot's theory. That Preacher Sam had refused to fight Frank Curtis. That he had tried to make a getaway and that Frank, crazy with blind rage and his love for the Rose of Tascosa, had shot the fleeing man in the back. And would rather die a hundred thousand times than admit it. That was Hipshot's theory and he bluntly stated it to Galt when the young cowboy cornered him into talking.

"If Frank Curtis got shot, it was after he killed Sam Magrath. Pecos or some of the others like Little Jack or The Cuter, who was with the San Saba Pool, shot Frank when he wouldn't join 'em. That's where Frank Curtis got the bullet holes that the Rose of Tascosa patched up in his hide. I know what the sign told me and what my common hoss sense tells me. You kin swaller that lie Frank Curtis tells. Not me. No man confesses a cold-blood, cowardly murder like the killin' of Preacher Sam."

Galt admitted the truth of that statement. But the killer was not Frank Curtis. Pecos Moss was the murderer who would brag of his gun notches but never admit the killing of the circuit-rider preacher. Pecos would have bragged of the killing of Preacher Sam to win the favors of the Rose of Tascosa. She had been trying to trap him into such a confession when he suddenly discovered her plan and shot her. And Galt figured that, under the right conditions, Pecos Moss would taunt Galt with the killing of his father. Because Pecos Moss was blaming Galt for a lot of his misfortune. The trick was to maneuver the dangerous killer into the right position where, certain that Galt would never live to repeat the confession, he would taunt the young cowpuncher with the truth about the killing of Preacher Sam. But only fate and a chance in a thousand would bring about such a thing. And Galt had little hope of clearing Frank of the burden of Hipshot's accusation.

"It takes a thief to ketch a thief," Spud Dulin chuckled. "Hipshot, you and Frank take what men you need and go after Pecos Moss and Lon Coulter and fetch 'em back alive."

The old cattleman wanted to take Galt back with him to the PD home ranch, but Galt balked.

"I've got to go with Hipshot and Frank."

"To keep 'em from lockin' horns, eh? But how about that shoulder of yourn?"

"It don't bother me," lied Galt. "I got to go along with 'em."

"And I'm too old to go on long chases," said Spud Dulin. "I'll stay here with what cattle we got gathered."

He told Hipshot to pick what men he needed for the man hunt.

"Me and Galt will do," said Hipshot. "Frank Curtis kin come along if he's a mind to."

"Me and Galt and Hipshot," said Frank Curtis, "will be a-plenty."

"The hell you say!" exploded Spud Dulin. "You don't know how many men will be with Pecos Moss. What kind of a fool play are you tryin' to work on me?"

"Me and Frank Curtis," said Hipshot, standing with his weight slouched on one long leg, his saddle rope coiled over one arm, "has both rode with Pecos Moss. We savvy his ways. You said it takes a rustler to ketch a rustler. . . . Rope your top circle hoss, Galt."

So Galt rode between Hipshot and Frank

as they left camp. They headed south, riding in silence. As dusk turned into starlight. The trail narrowed through a barranco spotted with brush patches. Hipshot called back over his shoulder to Galt, who rode behind him.

"Ask Frank Curtis does he figger Pecos will head for Tascosa or Dodge?"

"Tell him," sounded Frank's flat-toned voice, "that I figger Tascosa the best bet."

Galt grinned faintly. Had the circumstances been less grim, he would have gotten no little amusement from Hipshot's determination not to directly address the man he intended to kill. He was going to use Galt as a sort of human telephone, a silent interpreter.

"Pecos knows this country is too small to hold him," Frank went on, addressing his words to Galt's back, "because Spud Dulin has taken chips in the game. And no rustier kin hold a bunch together when they find out they're buckin' the PD outfit. Chances are every coyote in Pecos's pack has tucked their tails between their laigs and hauled freight for a safer climate. They've quit Pecos like he was poison to 'em. Pecos can't work alone rustlin' cattle. His one bet is to stick up some pay-day gamblin' game where there's gold on the table. Pull a fast hold-up and hightail it for a new range. Dodge is dangerous on account of Bat Masterson. There's damn little law right now at Tascosa."

"I figger," Hipshot broke the silence that followed Frank's words, "that this shirt-tail cousin of Frank Curtis's, this Lon Coulter thing, will be sidin' Pecos Moss."

"You kin inform the gent ridin' in the lead," called Frank, "that Frank Curtis ain't a damn bit proud to be claimin' Lon Coulter as kinfolks. But where we cut Pecos Moss's sign, we'll likely sight Lon. And Spud Dulin's orders is to take 'em alive."

"There'll be two-three tough hands trailin' with Pecos and Lon Coulter, tell him," said Hipshot.

"None of the San Saba Pool traitors will be with Pecos," called Frank. "The two that was with Pecos when he massacred the San Saba Pool men is dead. Little Jack and The Cuter. Hipshot killed 'em in Las Vegas."

"Tell me somethin' I don't know," snapped Hipshot testily. "I didn't figger I was just out fer target practice when I downed Little Jack and The Cuter. Four men rode away from there alive. Two of them four is still livin'. Pecos Moss is one. The name of the other is Frank Curtis."

"Ask him," said Frank, as a chill ran up

and down Galt's spine, "if he figgers Frank Curtis had any kind of a part in that massacre."

"Tell him," rasped Hipshot, "that I know damned well he didn't. Who brung up ary mention of the San Saba Pool, anyhow? What I'm sayin' is that Pecos Moss will have Lon Coulter sidin' him. And there'll be two-three other tough hands that didn't rabbit on him. Say there's four of 'em. Their plan will be to clean up Tascosa. The store and saloons and gamblin' games. Four tough men could do it if they played their cards right, and wasn't scared to do some killin'."

"Six would be handier than four. There'll be Pecos and Lon. And trailin' with 'em will be Pock Mark Smith, the Cherokee Kid, Deefy Brown, and Nigh Wheeler. That's my guess of the notched-gun tough hands of the Pecos Moss gang that didn't rabbit when Spud Dulin declared war on all rustlers and the Pecos Moss gang in particular. Them gents has all heard the owl hoot. None of 'em scare easy. And before they shot hell out of Hipshot's outfit about a week ago, this side of the Red River, they'd heard the rustlin' of the leaves that carried Spud Dulin's war talk. They never tried to gather the cattle they scattered. The PD riders will pick up the Mill Iron stuff without trouble.

Because the rustlers found 'em too laig-weary and footsore to travel fast and they dropped 'em. The renegades that was scared of Spud Dulin quit the country. But my guess is that Pecos kept them four gun slingers I named. And Lon will side Pecos because it's his one chance to make a fast stake and find a new range. Tell the gent up ahead that's my guess."

"Pass the word that it tallies with mine."

They pushed hard along the shortest trail to Tascosa. By hard riding they could make it before dawn. . . .

A round, white moon rode the star-filled sky above Tascosa. So that the six riders coming towards town could have counted the slabs marking the graves of the Boot-Hill, as they approached it.

Pecos Moss, riding with Lon Coulter, the other four trailing behind, reined up. From under the low pulled brim of his hat, his bleak eyes, bloodshot from wind and sun and dust, stared at a new grave, as yet un-marked. Leaning a little forward, his weight in the stirrups, hands on the saddle horn, he stared hard at the grave of the Rose of Tascosa. Then he rode slowly on, the shadow of his hat hiding a queer glitter that had crept into his cold, hard eyes. Lon and the others knew that the new grave held the dead body of the Rose of Tascosa. Not by so much as the lifting of his hat had Pecos Moss paid his last respects to the woman he had killed.

Where the main road entered the town, Pecos Moss again pulled up. This time to scan a notice nailed to a post at the side of the road. In the moonlight the large, black lettering was plainly visible. The sign read:

NOTICE and WARNING
TO PECOS MOSS, WOMAN KILLER
TASCOSA HAS A ROPE NECKTIE WAITING
FOR YOU
WELCOME TO OUR BOOT-HILL

"So this is where you are takin' us to raise a quick stake," said the tall man with badly pock-marked face. "I don't know about the rest of you gents, but I was always brung up to take a hint. Me, I don't want nothin' in Tascosa. Right here is where Pock Mark Smith turns back."

"Why, you dirty, yellow-bellied, gutless, rabbit livered —"

Pecos Moss, his face distorted with black fury, snarling, shot from the hip as the pock-marked man reined his horse. The heavy lead slug caught the man in the back, breaking his spine.

Pock Mark Smith's head snapped back loosely, and as his horse jumped, his long body flopped loosely and toppled sideways crazily. He must have been dead when he hit the ground with a sickening thud. Dust puffed sluggishly around the twisted shape on the ground. The riderless horse trotted off, head held sideways to keep from stepping on the dragging reins.

The eyes of Pecos Moss, greenish slits in the moonlight, glared at Lon and the other three. A thin wisp of smoke came from his gun barrel.

"Well?" he croaked harshly. "Speak up! How do you like it out West? Anybody else bothered with gut trouble?"

His eyes traveled dartingly from one face to the next. The swarthy half-breed Cherokee Kid grinned faintly and shook his head. Deefy Brown, bull necked, beetle browed, battered, shrugged beefy shoulders and struck a match to light his half-burned stub of cigarette. The wizened, gimlet-eyed Nigh Wheeler spat a stream of tobacco juice at the sign, staining it with brownish yellow. Lon Coulter, the blood drained from his handsome face, was the only one who spoke.

"When a man rides the outlaw trail, he plays his string out. We're wastin' time here, Pecos."

"Then dab your line on that damned sign and drag it into town. Let the carcass of that gutless thing lay where it is. Ride ahead."

It was the Cherokee Kid, in whose blood was a mixture of the bad in both races, who roped the sign post and dragged it along the dusty road. Deefy Brown and the Nigh Wheeler flanked him. Lon dropped back to ride with Pecos Moss, who from now on was giving no man a shot at his back.

Lon Coulter stole a furtive glance at the face of the killer. And was shocked into something that was fear mixed with a sort of horror and loathing.

He saw a face that was a gray color, with specks of white, foamy stuff forming at the corners of a lipless, twisted mouth. Pale, greenish, bloodshot eyes that were narrowed to thin slits. It was the face of a maniac killer. To Lon there was nothing human about it.

Lon would have killed Pecos Moss as he would have killed a mad dog. But he had not the nerve. It was a fear that made him feel weak and sick at his stomach, and moisture beaded Lon Coulter's forehead and wet the palms of his hands.

So they rode into the cow town of Tascosa in the white moonlight, just before dawn. Into the plaza that was a hundred yards square. Save for the largest of the saloons, the squat adobes were in darkness. Tascosa had gone to bed. All except those late revelers in the big saloon and gambling place.

It was towards those lights of the saloon that the five men who, until a few minutes ago had numbered six, rode. Every man of them with a hand on his gun.

XVII

Hipshot, Galt and Frank Curtis did not enter Tascosa by way of the main road that passed the Boot-Hill. So they did not see the dead body of Pock Mark Smith where it lay crosswise in the dust, blocking the trail.

They halted at the adobe of the Señora. It showed no light. Nor did she open the door to their rapping. They were standing there, undecided, when her black-shawled figure showed coming from the direction of the Boot-Hill. She was running. And it was a couple of minutes before she could whisper what she had seen.

She had gone to take a candle to burn at the grave of the Rose of Tascosa. She was on her way to the grave at the edge of the Boot-Hill when she had heard riders coming and had hid. And had not been more than a hundred feet distant when Pecos Moss had killed Pock Mark Smith.

"Even now, señor," she spoke rapidly in her own tongue to Frank Curtis, "the five who are left are in town. *Madre de Dios,* that evil one who killed our beloved Rose of Tascosa. I ran back to get a gun to kill him."

"There was a law officer from Dodge City," said Frank, "and a young señorita. Where are they?"

"They left but yesterday. With the black *negra* in a wagon. The señorita with the hair like the night without stars, she cried at the grave and —"

"We're losin' time," said Frank Curtis, swinging into his saddle. "Come on."

They spurred their horses to a run as they headed for the plaza, riding three abreast, Galt in the middle. But they did not ride into the open plaza. Instead, they reined up at an adobe corral behind the blacksmith shop next to the saloon, dismounted and left their horses there.

Five saddled horses stood at the hitchrack, bridle reins dropped to the ground. Range horses are broke to stand "tied" in that manner.

From inside the saloon came the sound of a rasping, harsh, croaking voice that was like the snarl of an animal ready to kill. All other of the usual sounds of the place were hushed.

"Line up with your hands high and facin' the wall!" barked the voice. "We come here to git all the gold in Tascosa and we're r'arin' to kill to git it."

"Slip the bridles of their horses," whispered Hipshot to Galt. "Pecos and the others is in there. There's a back door. Frank will guard it. The windows have iron bars. Nobody kin git out through 'em. I'll take the front door."

"And git shot down before you kin pull the trigger," snapped Frank Curtis. "First thing is to set 'em afoot. Then Galt takes the back door. You and me go in the front."

They reached the hitchrack. It took but a moment to slip the headstalls from the five horses and set them free.

"Listen!" whispered Galt. "Pecos Moss. He's — *talkin'!*"

From inside came the sound of that rasping, snarling voice.

"The rope was never made that'll hang Pecos Moss! Hear that, you curly wolves of Tascosa? I killed your damned Rose of Tascosa because she tried to trick me with her damned lies. She wanted me to tell her who killed her husband, Preacher Sam Magrath. So she could marry Frank Curtis and have me hung for the psalm-singer's murder. But I matched her, lie for lie. And let her keep on believin' Frank Curtis killed the Bible toter. She died a-thinkin' her lover done it. And now I want to meet Frank Curtis face to face and tell him that I killed Preacher Sam. I killed him because he knowed too much about my plans to wipe out the San Saba Pool. And I shot Frank Curtis and left him for dead, not twenty feet from where Preacher Sam's carcass laid. Then me and Little Jack and The Cuter wiped out the San Saba Pool. I'll tell that to Frank Curtis when I cut his sign. And I'll tell him how I killed Jeff Curtis on the Las Vegas trail. Then I'll kill Frank Curtis like I'm goin' to kill a few of you sign-makers of Tascosa. You, mister storekeeper, for one. And the robber that runs this joint. And the gamblin' man in the black coat. And one or two of you painted she-wolves that rob the pockets of drunks. You had a hand in that sign paintin'. She was your angel. She was one of you, even if she didn't peddle her shape to any man with the price —"

"You lie!" screamed a woman's voice.

A shot. And through its echo a woman's scream of agony. Then a voice that didn't belong to Pecos Moss. It was Lon Coulter who was hurling a challenge.

"You coward!" Lon's voice was brittle. Like steel breaking into bits. "You woman killer!"

Two guns roared at the same instant. Galt beat Hipshot and Frank Curtis to the door. Leaped inside. The glare of the lights inside blinded him. So that he could not make out which one of the men was Pecos Moss. And then a bullet struck him in the chest. He reeled and tripped over the body of the dead dance-hall woman. Went down.

Hipshot was slower than Frank Curtis. It was Frank who stood just inside the doorway. And he was shooting at Pecos Moss. Pecos, blood-flecked foam on his lips, ashen gray face twisted in a terrible, maniacal mask of hate, stood swaying on widespread legs, shooting from the hip.

Hipshot dropped Deefy Brown and the Nigh Wheeler as they started for the door, guns blazing.

The Cherokee Kid had grabbed one of the dance-hall women and, using her as a shield, backed towards the rear door.

Galt saw him. Saw the half-breed and recognized him as one of the Two Pole Pumpkin men he had run out of camp. Galt tried to pick his gun from the floor where it had fallen, but his arm was paralyzed, numb, helpless. He saw the leering grin on the half-breed's swarthy face. Through the haze of tobacco smoke and gun smoke, he saw the black eyes of the Cherokee Kid glittering. And then from somewhere to the left and a little behind Galt, near the end of the bar, there came the roar of a gun. And as if in the grip of some terrible nightmare, Galt saw the dark, swarthy face of the Cherokee Kid suddenly turn into a horrible mask of mangled flesh and bone and blood. The gun dropped from his hand and his other arm let go the woman who took a faltering step or two, then fainted.

"A bull's-eye, Gospel Galt. Not bad shooting for . . . a dying man. Pecos was right . . . I got a soft streak in me. Savin' you for the girl I . . . You owe me a Bible plantin' . . . Gospel Galt." And Lon Coulter's left hand lost its grip on the edge of the bar and he slid to the floor, his gun slipping from his hand.

Pecos Moss, an empty six-shooter in his hand, red froth bubbling from his open mouth, was literally dying on his feet. His slitted eyes, even as death glazed them, staring at Frank Curtis. Then Pecos Moss's spread legs gave way suddenly and he dropped in a heap, his right arm outflung, his hand gripping the gun that still pointed towards Frank Curtis.

Frank walked with slow, dragging steps across the short distance, and stood looking down at the dead man. Then he thumbed back the hammer of his six-shooter and sent the last bullet in his gun into the dead man's back.

"That," he said through set teeth, "is for Preacher Sam. That last bullet that cut your suspenders where they cross."

Frank's words ended in a rattling cough. Blood gushed from behind his clenched teeth. He half turned, his eyes looking at Galt. There was a smile on his face as he sank slowly to the floor. He was dead when old Hipshot, shoving his way through the gathering crowd, bent over him.

Then Hipshot lifted Galt in his arms and carried him to a large, round-topped card table. Sweeping cards and poker chips and money off the table with a gesture that, under circumstances less grim, would have been magnificent, the old range tramp gently lay Galt on his back and with hands that shook, tore at the buttons on Galt's bloodstained shirt and undershirt.

The numbness in Galt's body, especially his arms and legs, was leaving, and he felt a tingling sensation as he moved his fingers. A man pushed his way alongside Hipshot.

"I'm a doctor. Let's have a look —"

There was some blood that the doctor wiped away with a bar towel. And a large, discolored, widening bruise on his chest, around his heart. The doctor frowned, puzzled. Then he picked up a mushroomed lead slug and studied it, shaking his head. Then from the breast pocket of Galt's vest he fished a battered, broken tangle of metal and small cog-wheels and tiny springs that clung together and seemed fastened to a watch chain fashioned of gold nuggets.

"The bullet struck it," grinned the doctor, looking down at Galt, "and saved your life, undoubtedly. A composition metal case stopped the slug's force and deflected it along a rib."

"Gawdamighty!" gasped Hipshot. "The stem-winder I won off that tin-horn at Santa Fe. Gawdamighty, Galt. The stem-winder. Gawdamighty. . . ."

There are many graves along the old cattle trail out of Texas to the north. Most of them are lost graves, grass covered, snow blanketed in winter. Lost graves of almost forgotten men.

Other graves are marked. The grave of the pioneer trail boss Jeff Curtis has its monument of granite. With its simple inscription:

JEFF CURTIS
TEXAN

On the Staked Plains or Llano Estacada, a monument marks the spot of the San Saba Pool massacre. Spud Dulin had it put there when he took the money for the Pool cattle he bought from Galt and Hipshot, to the widows and mothers and sisters of the dead cowmen who had died there. Like Jeff Curtis's monument, it is a granite slab bearing the names of the dead cowboys.

Not far from there is the old wagon tire that Hipshot used to mark the grave of Preacher Sam. But also one finds the more permanent granite with an open Bible carved on it. And this inscription:

SAMUEL MAGRATH
*Whose voice preached
the Word of God
in the wilderness*

At old Tascosa, near the crumbling ruins of adobe walls where once stood the toughest little cow town along the cattle trail, within a stone's throw from the Boot-Hill where the bones of outlaws like Pecos

Moss lie buried, is a small enclosure of white picket stakes. Kept freshly painted by the old señora who is one of the few remaining persons living at the ghost town. Inside the little enclosure are the graves of the Rose of Tascosa and Frank Curtis. And this is carved on the large, wooden cross above the twin graves:

REST IN PEACE

Nearby is the grave of Lon Coulter. Marked:

A BRAVE MAN LIES HERE

Those are the graves we know that mark the old cattle trail that was ridden by brave men.

At Dodge City you will find records of such other famous frontier men. Any one who knows anything of old Dodge can tell you countless stories of that city's famous peace officer, Bat Masterson. And old-timers there will recall anecdotes concerning such characters as Doc Holliday. They will remember Conch Jones, Dog Kelly, the Hoo Doo Kid, the Nigh Wheeler, Light Fingered Jack, and the notorious

Mysterious Dave Mathers. Many others who took their drinks across the bar at the old Beatty and Kelley Saloon and perhaps were sobered up by immersion in the old well out front in the street.

Perhaps some old-timer will recall the wedding at the hotel when Nancy Curtis was given by Bat Masterson in marriage to Galt Magrath. Gospel Galt Magrath will be remembered because he ducked a barber in the water barrel and so won the everlasting and substantial gratitude of old Spud Dulin of the PD whose eyebrows the luckless Sport McAllister had, in a drunken moment, trimmed while the famous Spud slept off a jag in the barber chair.

A notorious old range tramp called Hipshot was best man at the wedding of Nancy Curtis and Galt Magrath. And after the ceremony he and Spud Dulin slipped away from the big celebration. To appear at Las Vegas, New Mexico, some days later. And when they showed up, fairly sober, at the PD home ranch, Hipshot bore an official-looking document signed by a long list of names that was headed by the Mayor's signature. This seal and ribbon-bedecked document, in no uncertain terms, proclaimed that Hipshot was an honored and respected member of the Vigilante Committee of the

SUBSTANTIAL CITIZENS of Las Vegas, New Mexico.

That document hangs framed in the house occupied by Hipshot at the PD headquarters ranch where he is Foreman.

Nancy and Galt live in the new adobe a stone's throw from the old ranch house occupied by Spud Dulin. Bossed and scolded and loved by Aunt Cloe.

Spud Dulin made Galt a full partner in the PD outfit and likes to boast that the PD is the only cattle outfit in the country that has a sky-pilot ramrod. And on the slightest provocation proves it by dragging Galt to out-of-the-way places to preach from the old blood-marked, buckskin-covered Bible. Gospel Galt and his Bible, at Spud Dulin's orders, must take care of all baptisms, weddings and funerals on the vast PD range. A range which old Hipshot, as foreman, insists takes in most of the United States and the best part of free range back in Ireland.

This story gives the old range tramp no name save Hipshot. For that is the only name by which even Galt knows his old pardner. Though in his boyhood he had a name which, after he ran away from home, he changed as often as he changed ranges. Until the cow camps labeled him Hipshot, because of his manner of slouching when he stood on his feet. And even Hipshot himself had all but forgotten his real name when fate crossed his trail with that of his older brother Sam. Preacher Sam Magrath. Sam, whom he had always fought with and never understood.

"Claim me as kinfolks," Hipshot had fiercely greeted the circuit rider when they met, "and I'll kill yuh. My own brother a fire and brimstone sky-pilot. God ferbid. They'll hooraw me outa Texas."

"I'm not apt to claim a whiskey-soaked range tramp cattle rustler as a blood brother," Preacher Sam had told him. "Go your sinful way and I'll go my trail as God wills it."

It was typical of Hipshot that he had never told Galt.

"Nancy," Galt has said more than a few times to his wife, "if it hadn't been for old Hipshot, none of this happiness could have happened to us. Looking back along the trail, I can see where it was Hipshot that kept me on the right trail, letting me think all the time that I was sort of reforming him. He taught me how to face life. He taught me a lot of things. The finest pardner a man ever had."

Galt Magrath never said a truer thing than that.

About the Author

Walt Coburn was born in White Sulphur Springs, Montana Territory. He was once called "King of the Pulps" by Fred Gipson and promoted by Fiction House as "The Cowboy Author". He was the son of cattleman Robert Coburn, then owner of the Circle C ranch on Beaver Creek within sight of the Little Rockies. Coburn's family eventually moved to San Diego while still operating the Circle C. Robert Coburn used to commute between Montana and California by train and he would take his youngest son with him. When Coburn got drunk one night, he had an argument with his father that led to his leaving the family. In the course of his wanderings he entered Mexico and for a brief period actually became an enlisted man in the so-called "Gringo Battalion" of Pancho Villa's army.

Following his enlistment in the U.S. Army during the Great War, Coburn began writing Western short stories. For a year and a half he wrote and wrote before selling his first story to Bob Davis, editor of *Argosy-All Story*. Coburn married and moved to Tucson because his wife suffered from a respiratory condition. In a little adobe hut behind the main house Coburn practiced his art and for almost four decades he wrote approximately 600,000 words a year. Coburn's early fiction from his Golden Age — 1924–1940 — is his best, including his novels, *Mavericks* (1929) and *Barb Wire* (1931), as well as many short novels published only in magazines that now are being collected for the first time. In his Western stories, as Charles M. Russell and Eugene Manlove Rhodes, two men Coburn had known and admired in life, he captured the cow country and recreated it just as it was already passing from sight.

We hope you have enjoyed this Large Print Edition. Other Thorndike, Wheeler or Chivers Press Large Print books are available at your library or directly from the publishers.

For more information about current and upcoming titles, please call or write, without obligation, to:

Publisher
Thorndike Press
295 Kennedy Memorial Drive
Waterville, ME 04901
Tel. (800) 223-1244

Or visit our Web site at:
www.gale.com/thorndike
www.gale.com/wheeler

OR

Chivers Large Print
published by BBC Audiobooks Ltd
St James House, The Square
Lower Bristol Road
Bath BA2 3SB
England
Tel. +44(0) 800 136919
email: bbcaudiobooks@bbc.co.uk
www.bbcaudiobooks.co.uk

All our Large Print titles are designed for easy reading, and all our books are made to last.